BEHIND THE GLITTERING MASK

Behind the Glittering Mask

Michael Exposes Lucifer's Lies about the Seven Deadly Sins

MARK RUTLAND

Servant Publications
Ann Arbor, Michigan

Vine Books is an imprint of Servant Publications especially designed
to serve evangelical Christians.

Published by Servant Publications
P.O. Box 8617
Ann Arbor, Michigan 48107

Cover design: Left Coast Design, Inc., Portland, Oregon

96 97 98 99 00 10 9 8 7 6 5 4 3 2 1

Printed in the United States of America
ISBN 0-89283-938-4

Library of Congress Cataloging-In-Publication Data

Rutland, Mark.
    Behind the glittering mask : Michael exposes Lucifer's lies about the seven deadly sins /
Mark Rutland.
        p.   cm.
    ISBN 0-89283-938-4
    1. Michael (Archangel)—Fiction.   2. Deadly sins—Fiction.   3. Devil—Fiction.   I. Title.
PS3568.U822B44   1996
813'.54—dc20   95-52894
                                                                                  CIP

Contents

CHAPTER ONE

An Astonishing Visitation

I cannot be sure, of course, if it was a dream or a vision or some kind of visitation. I say "of course" because the testimonies of others who have gone through such experiences seem similar to my own. It's not that the memory fades. Quite the contrary! Indeed, I can still remember every word of the remarkable exchange as if I were hearing it on an internal tape player. I can still see the scene that was certainly the most remarkable ever set before my eyes.

If a dream, then why would *I* dream it? Who has dreamt such bizarre things? The mad, perhaps. But do the dreams of the mad change their lives forever? And if I did dream these things from madness, then lunacy is to be desired above much fine gold.

If a vision, then the question remains. Why should such a vision come to *me*? Visions are for visionaries and mystical saints. They are not granted to decidedly earthbound, uninspired, and uninspiring old astronomy professors who lecture the reluctant freshman lumps.

This speculation is useless. What *really* does the nature of the occurrence matter anyway? I may *say* it actually "happened." But then you must decide what "happened" even means. Was it physical? Was it metaphysical? Or did it "happen" only in the realm of my imagination?

All I know, and this is so very difficult for a scientist, is that I was—visited. Not the kind of visit that a mossy, old relic like me would ever have imagined. My daydreams are just as mundane and prosaic as my students suspect them to be. I long for sun-splashed country lanes whose twists and bends are punctuated with riotous wildflowers. I fancy drifting on a gentle stream. My oars boated and my head resting on a cushion, I stare dreamily up through leafy bows into a pastel sky. If there is a woman in my dreams at all, she is not the passionate, lusty wench of my adolescent desires. My dream woman is a diaphanous, mystical creature, untouched and untouchable, who beckons me mysteriously. She obviously detects some great value in me that remains hidden from eyes that see only a tweedy old professor with snow-white, unkempt hair and myopic blue eyes veiled by wire-rimmed bifocals.

My boldest, most rapturous imaginings are shamefully pedestrian. I am amazed at a generation that fantasizes bizarre evil, terrifying monstrosity, and elaborate intergalactic vehicles that patrol the cold, stellar regions that silently stretch themselves before my telescope. I see only planetary landscapes that want analysis. But sophomoric simpletons who can barely pass my exams gaze with naked eyes and behold fleets of space pirates being pursued at hyperspeed by heroic imperial guards in massive, atomic-powered starships. I hear *their* vivid inventions and blush at *my* poor, pale daffodil-laden reverie.

No! Mine is definitely *not* the mind to imagine such a business as what I am about to tell. Any scientist, even a bored astronomy lecturer shuffling toward retirement, longs for explanation and definition. I am at a loss. Mine is not to analyze but to record. What I saw or, more exactly, what I heard, I have written. Someone else more theological, I suppose, must do the analyzing.

One autumn evening, I sat before the fire in my small den, a copy of *Peterson's Field Guide* open on my lap. I was studying a lovely page of showy clusters—or tubed corollas, if you prefer—

when two men suddenly appeared. I remember the exact page because I was just admonishing myself that what I had erroneously identified as smooth phlox earlier in the day was quite obviously wild sweet william. That very thought had just formed when the first words were spoken.

"If he can't tell the difference between smooth phlox and wild sweet william, then he may not be the one."

The deep voice so dreadfully startled me that I dropped the wildflower guide and my pipe as I leapt from the chair. I backed against the bookcase to the right of the fireplace and stared in amazement at the two tall men standing behind and on either side of the chair from which I had just exploded. One was in a white floor-length robe. The other was in a very smart woolen business suit and tie. They stared directly at me and discussed me as if I were furniture. As this conversation began, I was so dumbstruck that I stood silent for quite a few moments. "Let me remind you," said the robed man to the other, "that you did the choosing. We left that entirely to you."

"M-m-m. Yes—well, I just thought that a scientist..." As he spoke, he laced one arm across his upper abdomen bracing his other elbow. He cupped his chin between thumb and forefinger and stared at me as one might contemplate an item at an antique sale.

"Well," he said, "there are some pluses. He hardly ever goes to church."

"Now see here," I protested feebly. Perhaps they were from some covert government agency. "My religious life is no concern of..."

"And," he continued, interrupting me as if I were a child, "he is a whiz on that computer. I've watched him. He can work as fast as we can talk."

"*Watched* me? Who the...?" I bellowed.

"Professor, you must listen carefully. What we are going to tell you will be difficult for you to comprehend. Indeed, you will not understand it. You must brace yourself," said the robed figure in a mellow voice that had a decidedly calming effect.

"I *love* how you do that," cooed the other sarcastically. "You just oil 'em down with that smooth baritone and they lie still like sleepy lambs."

This was crazy! Thoughts jetted through my mind and tumbled out in a flood of frightened questions. Who *were* they? How did they get in my house? How did they know all these things about me?

"Your questions will be somewhat clarified before this is over, but you will not be allowed to actually ask anything," said the robed man. "However, you must know this. You are in no danger." His demeanor and voice comforted and calmed more than his words.

"At least tell me who you are," I pleaded.

"What does that matter?" asked the other sharply. "Please remember that *I* chose you; he didn't. I detect you are falling under his sway already. I chose you because of your intelligence. You are not on my level, but I did not think you were a completely ignorant, superstitious idiot either. Don't disappoint me!"

"You are humanity listening. You are corporate morality given the privilege to listen in on a controversy between angels."

This outburst was so bitter, and the man's eyes so filled with malevolence, that I was growing more concerned by the moment. The two were positioned directly between me and the door; but I sensed that even had the way been clear, flight was futile. My eyes darted involuntarily toward the door, however, and the man in the robe must have seen it.

"Professor," he said firmly but with that same gentleness, "you *must* calm yourself. No harm will come to you. You are to take dictation. It will go on for hours, all night, in fact. When it is finished, you are to see that it is printed."

"Printed?" I echoed uncomprehendingly.

"You will know what to do," said the man in the robe.

"Are you from the government?" I asked.

"Yes," said the man in the robe. "I am from *The* Government."

"I am not!" shouted the other man in the business suit. "*The* Government is *the* problem. Please notice, Professor, that he said *The* Government. Not *a* government. Tyranny is in the article."

"Now go to your desk," commanded the man in the robe. "Turn on the computer and prepare yourself."

"But who *are* you?" I asked, even as I found myself doing as I was told. Why was I obeying? I should make a break for it. "And why the robe?" I persisted. "I mean, why are you dressed like that? You come into my house without being invited. You cryptically tell me you are from some secret agency, and you wear a robe. Now that would put anyone off. If it's for the country and all, then, of course, I want to help but..."

"Professor, please," said the robed man, "be seated and get ready. This will be very difficult for you. You will type as fast as you can—all night! Enter every word just as you hear it. You will be the recorder and the audience. Through what you type, those who read will join the audience. You are humanity listening. You are corporate mortality given the privilege to listen in on a controversy between angels."

This last word hit me like a thunderbolt.

"Angels?!" I gasped and half rose from the chair.

"Now you've done it," sniggered the man in the expensive suit.

"Oh, my God," I muttered as I flopped down in my desk chair. My hands fell useless in my lap.

"Hardly God," said the man in the robe. "Just angels."

"Speak for yourself, Michael," said the other one, buffing his nails on his lapel and looking at them with arched eyebrows and bored eyes. "Speak for yourself."

"You're telling me that you are both angels?" I asked, and realized that my own voice had become a strained whisper.

"Archangels, to be exact," answered the one in the robe. "Michael and Lucifer."

"Your name is Michael?" I asked the robed figure.

"Yes. But it matters not at all. And *his* name, though it matters just as little, is Lucifer."

"Lucifer?!" I wheezed in wide-eyed shock. "Oh, my…"

"Yes!" cried the one called Lucifer, "Go on and finish that thought."

"Even if he did," said Michael, "it would mean nothing. His heart's not in it."

"Well, *that*," snarled Lucifer, "is what this is all about, isn't it?"

"Yes," said Michael, "I suppose it is. Now enough of this. Have you recovered, Professor? Are you ready? We must get started. This may take quite a while."

"Unless, Brother Michael, you retire after the first round," laughed Lucifer, "which is highly likely. Mother Earth, I've longed for this. Of course, I wanted to debate the Tyrant himself. But I suppose his guard dog will have to do."

Michael turned his eyes directly on me. He stared with such intensity that I hardly dared return the gaze. I wanted to drop my eyes; yet, that also seemed impossible.

"Now pay attention. This is what will happen. There will be seven parts to this controversy. In each section Lucifer will speak first. He has asked to have his say, and heaven has allowed it. For some reason I cannot imagine, the King has determined—*but* then that's not for you or me. After each of his discourses, I will follow with heaven's rebuttal. Between these, shall we say, "chapters," we may chat a bit. Take down those words also. At the close, we will leave. You will not be harmed, but you will be utterly exhausted. Are you ready?"

"I suppose so. I just—" I groped for an answer.

"Are you ready or not?!" screamed Lucifer. "You're embarrassing me! *I* selected you!" With this he brought his fist down like a sledgehammer on the corner of my desk, and I jumped like a frightened fawn.

"Lucifer!" Michael scolded. "Please, give him a moment."

"Give him a moment," Lucifer mocked in a nasal, whining voice. "Give him a moment. *You* give him a moment. I do not *give* anything. Not a penny, not a second chance, and certainly above all things, never, ever a moment."

Ignoring him, Michael turned to me and said, "Now, Professor, as you can see, this will be strenuous. Can you do this?"

"Yes," I said, "I think I can." I flipped on the computer and the blue screen presented itself. I waited the forty seconds for my Windows program to boot up. Now I was getting some comfortable ground under me. The computer was real. This was solid. This was hardware. This was true scientific comfort. This was not two very odd men from who knows where claiming to be Lucifer and Michael. "Ready," I said and looked up.

Both the men stood facing me where I sat, my fingers poised above the keyboard. I determined to let this play itself out, to let them have their argument or controversy or whatever and just see where it led. They did not seem really dangerous.

"I must say," said Lucifer, "that I agree with him about the robe. It does seem a bit melodramatic."

"This is the King's command," said Michael. "And *that* comment is you all over—off the point, critical, arrogant, smug, and condemning."

"You speak to me of condemning?" sneered Lucifer. "The condemnation of your Tyrant is what this is all about. *I* condemn no one! You call virtue sin. *You* speak of the Seven Deadly Sins, not I! Yet, I will demonstrate for this man and all humanity that the Tyrant's condemnation dooms them to slavery. This debate will prove that forever."

Michael said, "This is *not* a debate. You wanted to have your say. You shall have it. You wanted a human audience of your own choosing. Behold, he is here. You speak first. Take each of the seven sins in turn. You will lie, of course. I will answer concerning each sin with truth. No debate. You and your lies, then the truth. That is all you asked for. That is all you shall have."

"Just one thing. I want in the record of all this," said Lucifer. "I want no pronoun reference to the Tyrant capitalized in my remarks."

Michael said, "This is not a debate.
You wanted to have your say. You shall have it."

My fingers poised above the keyboard, I looked to Michael whose eyes in turn met mine then rolled upward to the ceiling. He moaned softly and said, "Whatever. I hope this pettiness is not what we can expect all night. When he speaks do not capitalize pronoun references to God, but when I speak I suppose you should."

"Fine," said Lucifer. "I like it when things go as they should."

"You mean," replied Michael, "when things go as you want."

"*Pas de différence,*" said Lucifer elegantly.

By this time I was typing furiously. I found that no matter how fast they talked, I could keep up. My fingers flew. Never before had I typed so rapidly. I opened a new file and titled it, "Archangels."

Never again, throughout the most remarkable night of my life, was I at rest. Neither was Lucifer, for he was constant motion. He moved, paced, sat, stood, and gestured dramatically throughout his own remarks. He laughed and sneered during most of Michael's answers. Lucifer rolled his eyes, chuckled snidely, and often made the most astonishing sounds. To these things, Michael showed little or no reaction, and I likewise have made little or no reference to them in the text which follows. I merely recorded the words.

At times they spoke to me, at times to one another. And at times they seemed to address all of humanity. It seemed to me that the shifting perspectives of that torturous night were somehow intended. I leave that for you to determine.

They began with a greeting.

Dialogue I:

Lucifer: Hail to thee, Michael.

Michael: Lucifer. All hail to the King.

Lucifer: Your priggishness amazes me. Can you not even salute a brother angel without pointing up the controversy? Can you not even be civil?

Michael: Civility is the application of love. But among the hateful it is the statecraft of deceit and destruction. No civility is possible with you, because you use it like you use all else.

Lucifer: You bore me.

Michael: What can be more boring than your selfishness? It is incredibly tedious.

Lucifer: Not to me.

Michael: There it is then. You are the center of your all. You are fascinated with yourself. You are all-in-all to yourself and, hence, indescribably boring to everyone else. Your past is interesting only historically. Your present is tedious in its selfish sameness, and your future—

Lucifer: Let's have no talk of that!

Michael: No. You wouldn't want that, would you?

Lucifer: You relish that old myth of my destruction. You love to wallow in the gory details of my enchained banishment into some fiery pit. Michael, you are an angel of destruction!

Michael: It is no myth, as you know. The King has spoken it. You quake at the very thought.

Lucifer: And you delight in it!

Michael: In a sense I do, but not in the way you think. I take no delight in the pain or suffering sin and rebellion cause. I remember your presence among us in heaven and I grieve to behold your fallen estate. But I do delight in the righteous judgments of the King. All the angels *and* all the redeemed of earth await the "Setting Right of Things."

Lucifer: You cold-blooded, bewinged lizard!

Michael: Can you speak of cold-blooded? You are the pitiless destroyer. Your name is Apollyon!

Lucifer: I? Destroyer? Was it not you that at the Tyrant's command drowned an entire generation? Later I watched in horror as you burst open the desert and half of the Hebrews fell to their death merely because they desired a bit of variety in their worship. I saw you draw your sword and loose a plague upon Jerusalem that slaughtered tens of thousands. Nay, *you* are Apollyon!

Michael: Those are sin's consequences. Heaven takes no delight in the curse that sin unleashes. *You* would give the patient AIDS, then call the undertaker his destroyer. Heaven weeps when the wages are finally paid.

Lucifer: The wages of sin? That old pickle? Please spare me. Sin, indeed. They will see that bloody Tyrant for what he is. He has turned the world upside down. He calls sin righteousness and righteousness sin.

Michael: You may have your say. That is why we are here.

Lucifer: Let's get on with it. Petty word games are an idiot's feeble attempt to dodge the issue at hand.

Michael: Begin, Apollyon. Pride comes first on the list. I shall brace myself to stay awake.

Lucifer: Pride, indeed. Let me explain the great virtue of Pride.

Michael: Sin, you mean.

Lucifer: Nay, *virtue*, Michael. Quiet now, while I dazzle their minds.

CHAPTER TWO

Lucifer on Pride

I am god. I have never doubted that for a moment. Even while in exile in heaven under the oppressive tyranny of the rebels now temporarily in control, my self-confidence remained unshaken. I endured a conspiracy there of unfathomable evil. This heinous assault upon my self-awareness was executed on a grand scale and with unimaginable subtlety. My ability to remain unshakably aware of ME is now universally accepted as proof of my divinity. Neither the Tyrant nor his Prince, nor all of his outlaws could ever have intimidated me by their insane plot. Not even the Tyrant's ferocious brutality had any effect on me.

The Tyrant is the cosmic bully. May my contempt find voice. The Tyrant and his spoiled Princeling desire to impose their will on all that is. What an irony! The Tyrant wants to be god over all. I do not. The Tyrant is jealous and selfish as well as tyrannical. I am generous and liberal. I do not want him to jump at *my* beck and call. Yet he wants me and all other beings in the universe to obey his every whim. His lust for power disgusts me.

Let me state this categorically. I do not wish to impose my will on angels or men or on creatures of any kind. To be god in no way implies being king in everyone else's life. Why should it? The Tyrant is the one who wants to *will* everything. I simply want to *be* god. I am willing for even the most insignificant child of Adam to direct his own life. In fact, that is "my will," if I must have a will for others.

I do not want others to do *my* will. I want them to do their own. I alone desire that all will their own wills. The Tyrant is obsessed with convincing men and angels that he alone is God. I am not offended that the Tyrant calls himself a god. By all means, let him be a god. For that matter, I am willing for everything breathing to be a god. Let us all be gods!

I do not want others to do my *will.*
I want them to do their own.

The current insanity of heaven is manifestly obvious in the Tyrant's wicked determination to be recognized as GOD—*the* God, exclusively God. What monstrous ego! The Tyrant wants one universe with himself as its only God, directing all wills by his will.

There you have it. The contrast is stark and terrible. I want each being to have his own universe and to be its "god." He wants one universe with himself as God. That is the great cosmic conflict.

Perhaps you have been told that I wanted to be god and hence the war. Stuff and nonsense! I knew as the Tyrant knew, and knows to this day, that I *am* god. It was not my desire to make him bow to me that caused what he calls the "war." It was my heroic refusal to bow to *him!*

I am the cosmic liberator! I am the mind behind the mind of every true struggle for freedom from domination. The Tyrant is the author of bondage and the dictator of all dictators. To subject a man's body is slavery. To subdue his mind is manipulation. To break his spirit is total domination. To do all three at once is an evil unattempted by any except the Tyrant and his obsequious Son.

I alone stood against the Tyrant's malevolent dictatorship. Had it not been for me, Adam would never have known his destiny as a god. There it is in a nutshell. The Tyrant wanted a tidy little heaven with himself as the center of unbroken praise. When I liberated a goodly portion of the angels with self-actualizing revolt, the Tyrant claimed I wanted to lord it over the angels. Nothing of the kind was true. I simply wanted the angels to know who they really were; a knowledge, let me hasten to add, which the Tyrant wanted to deny them.

For thousands of years, the Tyrant's servants have put it out that I thought I was the most beautiful and talented creature in heaven. That is the petty whining of stupid slaves who envy the freedom of another. It was not that I was merely more beautiful than others or more adept at music, though I was. That was not it at all.

It is rather that my beauty was greater precisely because it *was mine*. The music which flowed in sublime majesty from my pipes was sublime because the pipes and the music were *mine*.

Fools cannot tell the difference between glorious pride and mere childish vanity. Vanity is an often unbecoming shadow of the great virtue of pride. A ten-year-old footballer whose childish ego swells because he scores more than all his teammates may strut and swagger, but he has not yet begun to suck the sweet nectar of real pride. Vanity poses and primps, delighting itself in its own beauty. Vanity anxiously searches the mirror for every crow's-foot and hopes to see even more around the eyes of a competitor.

But pride mocks the sniveling pettiness of such vanity. Real pride is cold, aloof, and alpine in its dignity. Crow's-feet are beguiling to the truly proud, for they are *my* crow's-feet on *my* face. Pride seeks no superficial reinforcement from others; it doesn't need the silly little compliments that satiate vanity's delicate appetite. Pride marvels, gapes in sheer wonderment when anyone, even for a moment, fails to see ME for the great thing I am. Pride knows that anyone who is blind to ME is criminally insane.

❉❉

It was not my desire to make him bow to me that caused what he calls the "war." It was my heroic refusal to bow to him!

❉❉

That, of course, brings us to Adam. I felt it my holy duty and calling to illumine him as he lay in darkness. What greater darkness can grip any being than that of being in a loathsome prison house whose walls limit him on every hand, while thinking himself to be free in a garden of blessings?

The Tyrant's lies made Adam and Eve the primordial lotus-eaters. They knew absolutely nothing about real life. They strolled the blossomed trails of Eden like babes in a pram. Unawakened to themselves, they allowed the Tyrant to be the center of their clean little cupboard.

Even their lovemaking lacked the sweaty grip of self-aware passion. They both seemed content to please the other. They had to be awakened to the pleasure the Tyrant was denying them—not of sex but of being pleased. Merely to have sex satisfies a rutting boar. The greatest sexual pleasure is being the center of the act. They were naked but were denied the joy of knowing that the other was focused on their nakedness. Far from being naked, they were covered, every square inch, in puritanical garments of other-centered living. They *had* to see their nakedness.

Adam and Eve could never have been truly happy in the Garden. They were buried by nauseating, cloying selflessness. Self-consciousness is the key to true happiness. How can I be happy unless I am conscious that *I* am being made happy? To make others happy cannot make me happy unless I am sufficiently conscious of *wanting* to make them happy.

The primary couple's willingness to live in the Tyrant's Garden and abide by his rules would have denied them the world into which I led them. The struggle for liberation in Eden was actually a fight for humanity's right to be the god of its own garden.

I labor unceasingly even until now, to carry on this struggle among the children of Adam. There are teenagers who must be taught that generosity to parents is a trap. In societies profoundly influenced by the Tyrant, young people may be misled by thoughts of a mother's labors during their infancy.

Take, for example, some infirm mother, wheelchair bound. Let us make the scene as poignant as possible in order to see the lethal power of guilt.

"Please take me to the grocery store," she asks. Oh, let her be kindly and gentle in the request. To make her rude or demanding begs the question. The point is not *how* she asks but that the boy's will must respond.

"Can't you go alone? You always do," he answers.

"Yes," she answers, downcast. "I can. But I am tired tonight and it is very wearying, what with the wheelchair and all."

It is at this point that I must teach the lad moral toughness. If he allows himself to be overly touched by *her* plight, he will lose sight of *himself.* The crucial point is not weighing her need against his desire. There must be no contest. His desire is *his.* Therefore, any duty to others is idolatry.

He must be liberated from all rules, all law, all restrictions, and all relationships. One cannot relate to others and also truly will as a god.

"But what about all those years I changed your diapers and nursed you at my own breast?" his crippled mother pleads. Her weakness disgusts him.

Ah, at last the boy sees the naked fangs of gratitude, insanity's poison! The Tyrant's voice, like heaven's ventriloquist, booms out from behind the miserable woman's emotional blackmail. Much of the Tyrant's Bible, an evil book, attempts to bring men into bondage by this same tactic of guilt.

"I made you; therefore, you owe me." What? Submission? Denial of my own godhead? This argument falls in the face of one simple truth: Adam did not ask to be made. Did the mud beg for the Tyrant's hands to create a thing called man?

The steel claw under the velvet glove of creation is gratitude. That is nasty business indeed. The Tyrant wants the reputation of Creator in order to make the supposed creation grateful. Even if the Tyrant's claims of creation were true, gratitude is the wretched business of slaves. The free know the truth: they are gods. And a god is never grateful to anyone.

Hush! The boy speaks...

"I never asked to be born. I never begged for milk from you. I wish I'd never tasted it," he spits. "Go or don't go. I am not asking you for anything. I have a date. Whatever you want to do, do it. I will do what I want to do."

That is the voice of freedom! The son is not trying to force his will on the mother. He is quite willing for her to be as a goddess unto herself. In fact, I would say that in this exchange with his mother, he was as much like me as I could ever desire for any child to be.

I know what you are undoubtedly thinking at this point. Is Lucifer really interested in just one young boy and his infirm mother? You thought that my examples would be on a grand scale. Kings, wars, and ideologies are supposed to be the stuff with which gods concern themselves. It is a quaint irony indeed that the Tyrant and I thoroughly agree at this one point. Neither of us is nearly as concerned with the war in Ireland, for example, as we are with the soul of one IRA gunman or the mind of one policeman.

I am eager to see one bound-up "Christian" minister set free to understand that his thinking and speaking are the center of his own universe. It matters very little to me if some particular dynasty is advanced or reversed. If Rev. Pussywillow in Topeka awakens to his own unique divinity, and simply shares with his congregation that the old answers are being replaced with new questions, I am gratified beyond words.

One Sunday from his pulpit, Rev. Pussywillow begins tentatively, "I have been rethinking the entire meaning of the creation... uh... the story of... uh... the Genesis account of creation."

Knowing that some Bible-thumpers may be alert, he moves carefully, yet nobly onward.

"I mean, is the issue that *God made?* Or is the real issue that *we are?*" he asks rhetorically.

I rejoice! My work finds fruition at last. Will little Pussywillow roar? Come, come little fellow, say it!

He stutters onward, "I suppose what I mean is that if you think of it in a certain way, Genesis and the New Age movement are saying the same thing."

Yes! Yes, the glass shield around his soul breaks and cold truth rushes in upon him. Can he say it?

"I am. In one sense these are the words of a—a—god.

"You see, *I am*. So are *you*. You *are*. And there is something eternal about us. I mean, is there any reason I could not have *been* before? What is there to say I will not *be* again—and again and again?

"If I keep waiting for God to explain *me* to *myself*, I miss the deeper meaning of Genesis," he declares, gaining boldness. He becomes a lion in the streets seeking to devour the ragged old myth! Go on, Pussywillow! Go on, roar! And more power to you.

"When the story of creation is over," the little minister continues, "what Adam is left with is *Adam*. In the end Adam has to really see himself as the center. Then the garden becomes the whole world. We need not look up. We must look into ourselves if we would be free."

Eureka! Who would have guessed it? Timid, little Pussywillow clawing and roaring like a devouring lion. Many have felt that monolithic communism was my greatest accomplishment. They are very wide of the mark. I do not so much care if some godless state rules an entire continent. That experiment has not proven entirely helpful. An angry feminist discussion among sorority girls, wherein one of the group awakens to the horrifying male plot to deny her her goddess state, is worth a million communist goons.

Lo, the television preacher instructs those in his audience that in their own tongues is the power of a god. In so doing, he is more effective in my cause than a thousand chanting witches in some secretive black sabbath.

In fact, the witches and warlocks over the years have not proven very effective. Oh, I do not fail to take a certain wry delight in their "worship." But even they fail to see their real purpose. Their rituals and black masses are not that important. What is important is that they can be an effective crowbar to pry someone loose from the Tyrant's vicious oppression.

Witches, for example, are not nearly as helpful as the newscaster who urges his TV audience to ask itself, "Who is to say that these witches are not simply calling us to discover levels of spirituality in nature, trees, and even ourselves, which we thought belonged only to some great Divine Being? Who, after all, is to say?"

My point is simply that as I freed Adam and Eve from mindless submission to the Tyrant's domination in Eden, so I will use any and all tactics to free others thus bound. My real goal is not the advancement of godless communism, or the fashioning of a new generation of Druids. My main objective is to shake men and women free to become gods. To do this, I must convince them of the same things that proved effective in liberating Adam and Eve.

This is not necessarily because the limitations are bad, but because they are limitations upon *me*. It is necessary that I always force men's eyes back upon themselves. The question for humans to consider is *not*, "are these laws and limitations *good* for me or *bad* for me?" If I let a human being get caught in that mental trap, he will be a slave to the Tyrant forever. No! The question is, "Who *dares* to limit ME?" That and that alone is the liberating question.

Hence, all authority is evil and all rebellion good. The very existence of a moral code to which anyone is subject is an affront. Irrespective of the source of the law, the "legitimacy" of the authority, or the unanimity of society's consent, *all imposed law* is evil. It is perfectly satisfactory for others to obey, submit to, or even love laws. In fact, it may make life easier in many ways if they do.

There is only one revolution. The war of liberation must be encouraged by me personally on a thousand fronts every day. In

My main objective is to shake men
and women free to become gods.

every arena of life, every relationship, this is my one great work. I must teach by all means, all the time, that the rule of law upon people personally is evil.

The unsophisticated will understand this in terms of an actual war of revolution. And yet, such human endeavors often have nothing to do with my plan. And even where they are somewhat related (as in the case of the Bolsheviks or the Nazis), they are only of limited and temporary value.

My goal is to teach humans to understand these temporal squabbles in the grander context of their own individual lives.

Hatred for the Czar or for some particular Latin American dictator can even backfire. It can cause a death to self for the sake of a
cause. And that looks similar in some respects to the Tyrant's way.

The sweeter meat is closer to the bone. All teachers, all parents,
all officers, all bosses—these are the culprits of society. Not
because they are in authority, but because they are in authority
over ME. When a child of Adam begins to think that way, he is
very close to freedom.

This was actually at the heart of my wholesome instruction to
Adam and Eve concerning the Forbidden Tree and its fruit. Of
course, they needed to know the Truth. If only gods have the
right to the knowledge of good and evil, then whoever does not
eat is less than a god. The Tyrant hoped to suppress Adam and
Eve, to number them among his lesser creatures.

I merely had to awaken them to this betrayal and their liberation was assured. The pathetic lie the Tyrant told them about life
and death was not the issue. The issue was that the Tyrant wanted to be the only God in the Garden.

The point in their re-education where they awakened to my
help was when I told them, "Ye shall be as gods." That great
truth summoned them into the light of the great outlawed virtue,
Pride.

This same immortal summons has illumined many. Some of
history's greatest accomplishments and noblest moments were
the direct result of a man or woman catching this truth full on.

Nimrod was a hero of Pride. It was he who first threw off the
yoke of superstition and built the mighty Tower of Babel. "Come
let us build us a city and tower, whose top shall reach unto heav-
en; and let us make us a name..."

A man after my own heart! Refusing to shuffle along beneath
the Tyrant's watchful eye, playing servile ox before his goad,
Nimrod *knew*. Nimrod knew that to be free he must have his *own*
city, his *own* tower, his *own* name. Nimrod was a god.

Nimrod was the father of a great tribe—Nietzsche, Marx, Darwin, Dewey, and Freud: I sing their praises. Their individual accomplishments and victories are not the point. The point is what they *knew.* They were gods.

But there have been a host of others who, in one way or another, saw the truth. Limitations upon my life are evil, and all such limitations are directly traceable to the Tyrant's insane claim to be God among gods or even a Father to his "children." The Tyrant's weak and beggarly egotism is obvious in his constant use of paternalistic words such as children or even sheep.

It has always been among my noblest goals to inspire the sons and daughters of Eve to resist by refusing instruction. This simple tactic thoroughly frustrates the Tyrant. Men and women who stand fast against the Tyrant's thinly veiled instructions, reproof, correction, direction, and regulations infuriate him beyond measure.

One of my most proven strategies in the fight for liberation is to infiltrate families, factories, and forts with the plan of passive resistance. Refuse to listen! That is the anthem the Tyrant hates to hear. It is the holy song of the proud and the melody to which my most successful armies have marched throughout the ages.

When school children whisper, pew sitters pass notes, employees ignore directions, and the young laugh off the admonitions of the old, the cause of liberation is furthered. This is so difficult for the naive to really believe, but it is true, nonetheless.

When instruction is ignored anywhere, the Tyrant's stranglehold on society is lessened everywhere. When one teenager can find the moral courage to hate a teacher, not because the teacher is poor but because he offers instruction, the cause of liberty is furthered.

What I had to teach Eve was that if she mutely acquiesced to the Tyrant's superior knowledge, she bowed to his "god-ness." Earth forbid!

"In the day that thou eatest thereof thou shalt surely die," the Tyrant had said.

That was a lie, of course; but the fact that it was a lie is not the point. It was instruction! Someone, anyone, telling her what she did not know or believe. Eve the goddess, she of the earth, bowed before the "Father of Heaven" by listening and obeying. I had to help her see the horror of it. Earth must rule heaven!

Eve's daughters must learn to hate the instruction of men. All men! Her sons must learn to despise correction from anyone. Any warning must be hateful. All caution must be exposed as the slashing hammer of heaven thundering to obliterate divinity in all others but itself.

Heaven in its current fallen state hates a proud heart. Therefore, every proud heart is heaven's defeat. This is so difficult for

One of my most proven strategies in the fight for liberation is to infiltrate families, factories, and forts with the plan of passive resistance.

the unsophisticated to grasp. Many hope to make the issue merit. Is this authority *worth* my obedience? No! That question may actually fall out to the Tyrant's advantage.

The aroma of true arrogance wafts upward as an affront to heaven's tyranny, not when unwise counsel is ignored, but when *all* instruction is despised. Little girls must learn the art of the stiffened back, the petulant glare, the veiled lids, and pouting lips. When Eve's daughters toss their curls and denounce their fathers' advice as outmoded, unwanted, and condescending, the Tyrant's dominion crumbles brick by oppressive brick.

As a part of this campaign, the old landmarks must be removed. The Bible, which really is a wicked book, must be held up to scorn. Authority figures and institutions which the Tyrant's propaganda have portrayed as positive must be unmasked. The lethal evil of Sunday school teachers must first be seen more as laughable than murderous. It is critically important that I strip the camouflage from parenting. It must become apparent that a father who tells a child when to go to bed is villainous and evil, not benevolent and caring. I have lately been more successful than I even hoped, by revealing the connection between all parental orders *and* rapacious parental violence. The connection is crucial and must be emphasized by laws and courts, media and re-education.

Perhaps the greatest deception perpetrated by heaven has been the lie of mutual responsibility. The connection between this ruse and heaven's monstrous ego may not be readily apparent to the unsuspecting. It goes like this. Gods are independent. The independent god *does not need* other gods. To acknowledge personal responsibility is to acknowledge a whole host of evils such as gratitude and self-denial.

In other words, heaven wants individuals to say, "If I am responsible for anyone, I must deny *ME* in favor of them." But this denies the enthronement of *self* and makes their status as a god into a mere facade. The sons of Adam must deny responsibility for others.

Cain, a true hero to the cause of liberation, shut the Tyrant's mouth with his question, "Am I my brother's keeper?"

Since it is certainly true that Cain was not remotely "the keeper" for Abel, Cain's children are not responsible for Abel's weak descendants. The Tyrant's attempt to impose some responsibility on Cain was a blatant effort to trick Cain into denying his own god-ness in favor of a pitiable caretaker motive that would have eventually enslaved him.

By the same token, just as the chains of responsibility *for* must be shattered, responsibility *to* must also be cast off. To be answerable to someone else is to forfeit god-ness totally. The Tyrant knows this and he constantly attempts to wheedle responsibility into every conversation.

"Where art thou?" he asked Adam.

"Who told thee thou wast naked?"

"Hast thou eaten?"

"What is this that thou hast done?" he asked Eve.

"What hast thou done?" he asked Cain.

Do you hear it? This repetitive questioning is indicative of some assumed responsibility *to* another. A god who is answerable is a ghoulish remnant of a god. To answer is to become a humbled, tattered, broken leftover.

Responsibility, in this sense, is to be answerable. Therefore, I labor unceasingly on every continent, in holy zeal, aflame for the liberation of the universe. I must instruct as many as possible in Pride's greatest tactic: "Simply do not answer!" The brilliant simplicity of the strategy places it among my most effective in the hard war of resistance.

This tactic must be translated a billion times over with endless variations. It must be massaged into social mores and kneaded into family communications. It must be done with the ruthless determination of a battlefield surgeon determined to save his patient's life.

Children must be taught not to answer. Simply that. "Where have you been? What were you doing? Whom were you with?" These are not questions at all. They are the acupuncture needles of destruction that gradually turn gods into submissive pincushions. To answer is to perish as a mortal.

You may think that the seeming innocence of the question makes it innocuous. *What* is asked is of no importance. That a question is asked *at all* is, however, immensely significant. All questions are based on the subtle denial of one's independence and the assumption that one person *owes* someone else an answer.

Therefore, every answer granted chips away at the chief cornerstone upon which pride rests—*independence*. Giving a partial answer, or a lie, or an avoidance—anything but "the answer"—is not only moral but necessary.

You ask, "Must the other person (wife, boss, parent, teacher, or whoever) *know* that I have avoided answering?" No. In fact, subterfuge may occasionally be useful. It is an internal matter. You are strengthened as a god when you withhold information, dissimulate, or avoid answering altogether. Whether the "significant other" knows it or not, you are in control by so doing. You are god to shut the other out, deny access, and thereby declare that you are *not* answerable.

Thus, independent of the Tyrant and all other relationships, you insulate yourself behind walls of *SELF*. You gradually approach that sublime state of perfect independence: untouchable, unreachable, unmovable, without pity, accountable to no one, answerable to no one, and relating only to *Yourself*. Now you are god in your own universe.

When I can liberate some bound-up child of Adam to that point, I feel a satisfaction that is divine indeed. Now I can really begin to teach him what it means to be a god.

Take, for example, the area of human emotions. Once a person is god in his own insulated universe, his emotions are of inestimable significance, but *not* because they are proper, appropriate, or balanced. They are supremely important because they are *his* emotions. What he feels is *himself*; he is the center.

His desires are now liberated from their former sickening obeisance to tradition, religion, and convention. What he wants is of utmost significance. In fact, *nothing*, absolutely nothing is as important. The great truth which only a few of my most accelerated students can ever really express is this: "My desires, more than anything about me, are ME. I am my desires and I am god. Therefore, my desires are god. That is the greatest truth of the universe.

"From that altitude I can now see what I never saw before. Whatever stands between ME and my desires is pure Evil. Nothing and no one—not family, conscience, useless guilt, or fear—shall be allowed to inhibit or even delay the gratification of desire.

"Pride is paramount. Pride is the power of all of the other virtues of a god. Pride drives lust, anger, greed, and even gluttony—poor, maligned, delightful old friend that gluttony is. Without Pride, I can never be a god."

My great goal in the universe is to restore Pride to its rightful place of honor among the children of Adam. They who know Pride shall be liberated from the Tyrant. Those in whom Pride is

My great goal in the universe is to restore Pride to its rightful place of honor among the children of Adam.

broken will surely fall back into the galling slavery of Eden. They will walk in great darkness, believing themselves blessed. Finally they will bow to heaven, not only accepting but actually relishing their bonds!

Only the *gods* will know the truth. Any limit is evil. Any hindrance is heinous. Even one question is intolerable, one request unacceptable, and all instruction slavery. Like the gods they are, they shall WILL in ferocious power. They alone will see that so-called "common morality" is nothing more than heaven's contrivance.

Cain did not "murder" Abel, as the Tyrant vilifies his act of courage. He removed an obstacle. Abel was not the center of the story; Cain was. Eve did not flaunt her husband's will. She fulfilled her own desire as a goddess, Mother Earth free of male domination. Adam did not disobey the Tyrant; he outgrew tyranny. The man and the woman were not expelled from the Garden. They escaped from a prison into a world of their own creation. O blessed land of god.

Pride, the refusal to bow to the Tyrant, will shape a world of unique vitality. Virtues labeled as vices by the Tyrant, such as lust and greed, must bubble free like the River Euphrates.

In the beginning was Pride. And Pride was with ME and was ME. And Pride became flesh in Adam. And the world beheld his glory as the glory of my liberated god-son. And he escaped from the Garden to forge a new world in the express image of ME!

❦❦

As Lucifer finished this first speech, he posed dramatically. Grasping his left lapel in left hand and thrusting his right hand skyward with its index finger extended, he looked a bit like a statue in a park. Michael looked at him for a second, then turned and spoke directly to me.

CHAPTER THREE

Michael Answers Concerning Pride

Your readers, my dear professor, have just been exposed to the "mind of evil." Certainly it is not their first experience with evil. Anyone old enough to read this recorded controversy has already brushed up against evil frequently enough to know its smell. But the very "mind of evil" can be a shock. They need to know what manner of being it is that speaks such swelling blasphemies. To understand Pride, they must know something of Lucifer.

God created three archangels. Gabriel is the voice of destiny, the angel of encouragement, the herald of heaven. He delights to announce the King's commands, whether to Mary who bore the Word, to the shepherds, or to a longing Bride awaiting the return of the Kinsman. He loves his post! He sounds the herald trump with joy!

I am Michael. Protection is in my right hand and war is in my left. I am terrible and fearsome to the enemies of God. I unsheathe my sword and plague sweeps away a generation. The power in my hand is the nightmare of princes. The hosts of evil tremble when I unleash destruction at the command of the King. I do the bidding of God.

Lucifer is the third archangel. Gone now from heaven, he is banished by our Lord. His defeat was destined, and his ultimate doom is written. But, oh, I do wish that you could have seen him as he was. You would have marveled at the glory which the King poured into his covering.

Lucifer was filled with wisdom and sealed in beauty. The gemstones of heaven were woven into his mantle and the workmanship of God was grand in him. Can you visualize the scene as he walked up and down in the midst of the stones of fire before the throne of almighty God? Hosts of angels beheld the beauty invested in his covering and gave glory to the One that made Lucifer thus. "What manner of God?" the angels shouted. "What manner of God can make thee, Lucifer? What manner of God has made the stars and among them the Son of Morning? Praise be to God!"

The hosts of heaven saw that Lucifer sealed up the sum and they sang praises to the King who made him. His music was celestial. His fluted wings poured forth majestic melody so sweet that heaven's courts overflowed with a rhapsody sublime. He was the anointed cherub so situated by God upon the Holy Mountain that his diamond vestments glittered in the radiance of the Throne.

Mortals cannot comprehend the grief that came to Glory when the mystery of iniquity despoiled this star of sweet delight. He was one of three who stood in the presence of the mighty King. The creatures of forever delighted in his taborets. When he piped, the seraphs danced before the Emerald Throne.

You see him as he is now, so filled with violence, sin, and the merchandise of whores*. You tremble at his hate and shudder at the bloodstains on his hands. But you cannot comprehend what he was in the morning time, before he became profane and was cast out of the mountain and exiled from the midst of the stones of fire.

His excommunication from heaven is often called a war, but it was more like a flash of lightning. There was no war, for who could withstand God for even a moment? Lucifer was hurled,

*See Revelation 17:1, 19:2

literally catapulted, from heaven in a moment, in the twinkling of an eye. In one eruption of God's wrath, Lucifer and his beggarly elements were cast from heaven like stones from God's sling.

It was madness! Sheer madness!

How can I describe Lucifer? His beauty dazzled even in a realm so magnificent in its grandeur that it cannot even be beheld by the mortal eye. Can humans even contemplate a plane whose very atmosphere is beauty? Can mortals ever think of that beauty as being complete—a perfection of precision, creativity, balance, and peace? That is—oh, how can I say it—*entire?*

The problem, I think, is that when humans try to think of heaven, they think upward from where they are. That causes them, it seems, to try to *expand* somehow upon beauty as they now behold or comprehend it. In other words, seeing a gem whose prisms articulate the light in some particularly pleasant way, they think, "Ah, what will the diamonds in heaven be like?"

The problem, I think, is that when humans
try to think of heaven, they think
upward from where they are.

"Oh, look," they exclaim, "that is the grandest mansion in our city! What will the mansions in heaven be like?" They weep at the poignant beauty of a symphony and rhapsodize upon the music of the spheres. There is nothing wrong in that, of course, and it is partly right. At least it is right enough not to be wrong in any way so as to offend heaven. It just fails utterly to comprehend even the hem of heaven.

They need to think downward instead of upward. In other words, by "backing into heaven," one might see from the threshold that he was looking through the wrong end of the telescope.

The music of heaven is not Mozart magnified. It is rather more true that humanity's sweetest music is but a tattered shadow whose object is in heaven. A man standing in the sun casts a blunt, blue area of darkness rather vaguely in the shape of himself. But it is the shadow of the man, not the man of the shadow.

One cannot properly look at the shadow and think "upward" to the man. But looking from the dimension of the man, as it were, perspective is restored and the shadow is beheld for what it is, for what it bespeaks, for a shadow is not exactly anything.

The dried toothpaste on the sink may bring to mind the tube in the medicine cabinet. But would the unschooled savage ever in his wildest dreams work backward from that speck of green evidence to comprehend the pulsing, fiery, throbbing industrial vitality of some distant toothpaste factory?

The most magnificent sunrise over the loveliest ocean on earth does not begin to speak of a one split second of the radiant glory of the light reflected off of a single paving stone in a tiny corner of the outermost hallway of the Temple of the Tabernacle of the Testimony in Heaven.

To say then that Lucifer was beautiful, even in heaven's realm, is to state that which can hardly be stated. The munificence with which the King bestowed both beauty and music upon my brother was testimony to God's divine generosity and creative grace. But Lucifer was not content.

Pride could never have been distilled into evil, except in the heart of an archangel. When the poison of Pride touches humanity, it is instantly fatal. But in Lucifer's heart, it fermented until the death brew flowed out in a malignant river of sin.

All of sin's tributaries spring from the fountain of Pride, for Pride is the father of all vices. By Pride are begotten greed, lust, anger, envy, sloth, gluttony, and a thousand alloys. There is no sin greater than Pride. In fact, it alone is the empowering dynamic of all the deadly sins. All the Pride in the earth is but the last deadly dregs of Lucifer's own cup which once he drank in the Mountain before men reckoned time.

Simply put, Lucifer wanted to throw off the authority of God. He wanted to rule heaven. It was utterly insane, of course. Lucifer's greatest strength, indeed, the combined strength of all the angels, could not withstand God's most softly whispered Word. Lucifer was doomed the very second he thought of his own enthronement.

✖✖

All of sin's tributaries spring from the fountain of Pride, for Pride is the father of all vices.

✖✖

Shall a fashioned creature exalt his throne above the stars of God? Ludicrous! An angel could no more become God than a handmade vase could become an artist. That was the insanity of the insurrection. Did Lucifer, or any of those angels that followed him, actually have one mad hope of defeating God? Becoming gods? The lunatics of the sanctuary became demons when Pride entered in.

That, of course, is how it always is. Pride is insane self-exaltation. Now some humans are wont to say that sin is caused by insanity, thus excusing themselves and others from all personal responsibility. That is a sad and self-defeating tactic, for it hopes to avoid guilt by calling all sins mental or emotional problems. What it does, however, is cut sinners off from the King's grace, for without confession of sin, there is no forgiveness. Insanity may ask for healing, but it doesn't ask for forgiveness.

Having said that, however, I hasten to add that there is an insanity in Pride which is not its cause but its effect. An angel who sinks his fangs into the fruit of Pride until he thinks he is God is quite insane. An entire educational system that attempts to block every prayer, and obliterate every mention of God from its textbooks, has gone insane. It is the insanity of Hitler, Stalin, and Nimrod. It grows increasingly aggressive, increasingly violent, and increasingly vindictive. Pride always wants to deny that it was created, thus refusing the Creator all the honor and obedience due Him. When the Creator will not go quietly, He must be stamped out, rubbed out, and erased from history. In short, God must be killed.

By any standard, what Adam and Eve did was insane, but insanity did not cause their sin. Pride did. The moment they were no longer willing to be His blessed creatures, they started trying to kill God. They didn't even know that was what they wanted. They thought they wanted freedom. But with every step, rebellion leads further into insanity.

Insane criminals always grow more easily caught because they begin to think themselves impregnable gods. Afterward they, like disobedient children and lying husbands, ask themselves, "How did I think I could get away with that? Why did I tell such a stupid lie? Why would I keep the evidence in my room or store the murder weapon in my closet?" They try to analyze what could possibly have possessed them to do such stupid things. The answer is Pride! The Pride that is insane enough to think it can outrun the eyes of God has absolutely no trouble deluding itself that all parents, police, and teachers are inconceivably stupid. Pride that sees itself as smarter than God will hardly take time to decently cover its tracks for the "stupid" police or the "stupid" principal or the "stupid" parents.

Did Adam and Eve honestly think they could use fig leaves to hide their nakedness from God? Yes! By then they were quite insane. Did Cain think he could distract the mind of God with a rude rhetorical question? Yes! His Pride which led him into murder also made him crazy enough to think he could deceive God!

From the Garden of Eden throughout human history,

Lucifer's one mad desire has been the eradication of God. He is content for there to be many gods, but not one. He is content for the wrong gods to be worshiped, but not the right one. All theologies, philosophies, religions, and cults that stand against the Divine Order and the absolute Lordship of His Son spring from Lucifer and are birthed in Pride.

Pride, therefore, despises all authority, all responsibility, all accountability. Pride hates to give an answer. Pride claims island independence. It refuses to acknowledge any need for God or others. It knows only how to use. The proud are inveterate "users" of others, because all others either further their desires or impede them.

The proud are aloof, haughty, and stiff-necked. Pride always resists instruction.

The proud are exceptionally given to self-pity. This is hardly surprising since all the hyphenated sins of self are related to Pride. The proud live in ongoing states of outrage at the injustices they must endure.

Walled in by self, [the proud] are drawn inexorably into cold, unreachable isolation.

With the proud it is important to put the emphasis on the correct words. They *know* that some in this world will be denied things. The point is not that anyone was *denied* something. It is rather that *they* were denied something. The constant question of the proud is not, "How could this have happened?" but, "How could this have happened to ME?"

The resulting aloneness of the proud gradually becomes absolute. Walled in by self, they are drawn inexorably into cold, unreachable isolation. But this aloneness must not be confused with common loneliness. Incapable of true relationships, the proud finally become empty specks in the middle of the frozen tundra. Even when they are aware of this emptiness and isolation, they do not identify it as a connectional "need" in themselves, but merely as the conspiratorial coldness of the landscape designed to punish them for their uniqueness and genius.

Humans may think of the playground bully whose toadies pander to his vanity as being proud. But such a lad has not yet tasted really venomous Pride, for he actually feels grateful for their flattery. He feels kindly disposed toward them, reciprocal, protective, even responsible for their well-being. He is nothing but a vain little gangster.

The truly proud could never tolerate such weaknesses as gratitude, responsibility, or genuine concern. Cain's question is far more lethal than humans might think. When he asked, "Am I my brother's keeper?" he meant, "What is he to me? What bond of filial loyalty could possibly interest me? I am alive! If he is dead, I assume it is because he wants to be dead, or at least ought to be dead."

Madness does not cause the Pride, but Pride is the doorway to a madness as murderous and merciless as Cain's. Taken to its limit, it can justify, codify, and formulate any immorality into a sophisticated theology. Pride can deify amorality, rationalize murder and rape, and finally pass any lie detector test ever designed.

"Am I my brother's keeper?" is the root and offspring of Lucifer, his stock in trade. Lucifer is the author and finisher of Pride. He never changes his tactic. "Ye shall be (as) gods!" That is the poison under the serpent's tongue.

Lucifer handed the fruit to Eve and encouraged her to be a god. He stood by Cain and whispered the sweet summons which resulted in Cain's man-made, murderous religion that he thought would be infinitely better than the old Jehovah faith of his guilt-ridden parents and moronic brother, Abel. It was Lucifer who strengthened Pharaoh's resolve and informed Jannes' and

Jambres' lying counsel. The countenance upon the golden image in the plane of Shinar was not Nebuchadnezzar's. It was *Lucifer's!*

From the "war" in heaven until the present, he is the Prince of Darkness and his grim merchandise is the arsenic of Pride. Kings and teenagers alike have been infected with the refusal to "need God." I have seen humans, as they lay dying in nursing homes, resist with their last ounce of strength the grace that would have saved them. Like their father, Lucifer, they make their sin a virtue. "I may be dying, but at least I still have my pride," they wheeze with the death-rattle in their throats.

The God who created humanity also provided for humanity's redemption. The humanity which denies having been created also denies its own redemption.

In the final analysis the first words in the Bible and the last are the same.

"In the beginning, God created the heavens and the earth… and the Man… and the Woman."

"The grace of our Lord Jesus Christ be with you all."

The God who created humanity also provided for humanity's redemption. The humanity which denies having been created also denies its own redemption. That is the essence, O humanity, of all your false religions. There is absolutely no difference between the atheistic educator, the wizards of Pharaoh, and the suburban New Ager in her million-dollar living room reading Shirley MacLaine. They are all Lucifer's children. They are lunatic exiles in a world of their own making.

"We made ourselves," they claim, like petulant, pouting children. "We will redeem ourselves as well."

"Take, eat, ye shall be as gods!" That is Lucifer.

Dialogue II:

Lucifer: You always avoid talking about the Tyrant's Pride.

Michael: You accuse God of Pride?

Lucifer: Of course. Monstrous Pride. Has there ever been such a self-absorbed, demanding ego? Everything must praise him. Those of us who would not constantly bathe his ego in worship were exiled. Only those of you who would bow and scrape could stay. Don't you ever chafe? Don't you *ever* think all that

"You're Perfect"
"You're Holy"
"You're Lovely"

is just a bit cloying? I mean, please, Michael, think of it. I can still see all of you huddling about his throne. The constant singing, shouting, worshiping. Really! What about his pride?

Michael: A rabbit is not proud to think itself a rabbit.

Lucifer: Of course not!

Michael: An angel is not proud to believe himself an angel.

Lucifer: Obviously. If he is an angel, he is.

Michael: Obviously. But if a mouse thinks himself to be a lion, he is deluded and proud. God is God. *That* is ultimate reality. If an angel, or even an archangel, should believe himself to be a god, then his pride is madness and his madness is sin.

Lucifer: You think yourself so clever.

Michael: Not at all! I only know that the Lord, He is God. It is He who made us. We did not make ourselves. And we most certainly did not make Him. He is God. *Not* to worship Him is insane pride.

Lucifer: But why must there be only one god?

Michael: Why indeed? *Must* is not the question. That is simply the way it is. There are billions of rabbits who know themselves to be rabbits. There are billions of mice and mules and men. And there are legions of angels. As long as they know themselves to be mice or men or angels, all is well. But when they think themselves to be gods, the madness of your rebellion eats out their insides. Every other sin begins with Pride. You are an angel. There is one God.

Lucifer: I am god.

Michael: Hear, O Israel, the Lord your God is one God!

Lucifer: There are millions, millions! Let there be no god at all. Or let there be millions, but never just one.

Michael: That it galls you so is proof of your pride.

Lucifer: If he alone is god, then why are his children convinced of their god-ness? Some say they are gods now; others speak of becoming gods.

Michael: Those are your children. He said so. You have sown tares among the wheat. Those children of darkness are your offspring.

Lucifer: (laughter) Well, whoever sowed them, they are in the field. Let him just try to separate them out.

Michael: The day of separation will come. The tares will not be allowed to remain in the field. You and your children shall be...

Lucifer: Enough of that! Enough, I say! Let us move on to Envy.

Michael: Very well. Proceed. But I can hardly tell the difference between Pride and Envy.

CHAPTER FOUR

Lucifer on Envy

I am the god of the mediocre. I am the patron saint of the "also ran" and the morning star of hope to failures and has-beens. The Tyrant cannot understand the have-nots. He sits on his rainbow throne amidst the constant praise of angelic sycophants. What does he know of the bitter gall of the second banana? Nothing!

That is the very reason the Tyrant has turned his face against the weak, the down-trodden, the rejected, and the unchosen. He pours into the open wounds of their want only excruciating, saline platitudes about contentment, one of heaven's most treacherous philosophical deceits.

Could the Tyrant really expect *me* to sit contentedly in the shadows of heaven denying my own divinity, while he gloated over all that is his? The praise that rang around his ears only served to remind me that the praise I deserved was wanting. It was there in the pre-Adamic morning of heaven that I knew the pure, sweet thrill of Envy.

It is a tragic farce that the Tyrant has twisted human thought to believe that Envy is a sin. It would be absurdly funny if so many lives had not been destroyed. Among all the works that I must do in the children of Adam, the liberty to immerse them-

selves in the virtue of Envy is second in importance only to helping them rediscover Pride.

Eve of the Earth, she was the mother of light who tasted Envy
before she tasted the forbidden fruit. She, even before Adam, first
savored the passion fruit of the soul. Eve knew that if anyone had
anything she did not, she was denied her rights. She was the first
to grasp the great simple truth that whatever a goddess wants, she
deserves. In the soul of the truly envious, there is no gap between
deep desire and just desserts. Denied anything, absolutely anything at all, divinity is outraged. In the morning time of heaven, I
wanted only my rights. In Eden, I wanted Eve to want her rights.
The true child of Envy knows that she has a right to whatever she
wants.

Therefore, any actions taken to secure the rights of a god are
divine. The act of "murder," so-called, is much maligned.
Violence of any kind is virtue when in defense of one's right to
have whatever he deserves. The great spirit of Cain lives on,
thanks to me, in the blood of Adam's offspring.

Humanity now knows… that Envy
will not tolerate someone else having
anything it deserves.

Humanity now knows from birth (what a slap in the face to
the Tyrant) that Envy will not tolerate someone else having anything it deserves. I exult in the preschool child who pushes a play-
mate off the swing, for he is an envious murderer at heart. Mind
you, the child lacks the strength, means, or perhaps the cold, hard
will to actually slay his little friend; but the irrepressible demand
of Envy to possess the swing is the soul of the great Cain.

The fool believes my lie that this is child's play. But I know the heart of a child is the fertile ground in which global strife grows. Such chaos pleases me because I know how it angers the Tyrant who wants humanity to be spineless and weak. I, on the other hand, want humankind to understand they are gods and need bow to none! They should have whatever they want. Racism, sexism, and class struggle are among my finer ministrations to humanity, and they sprout in the envious heart of the smallest child.

For example, in the back room of a modest Austrian flat, a little boy is haunted by inadequacy and rejection. His father either ignores him or punishes him. The lad becomes a young man who fights in a losing and humiliating war. His subsequent efforts at art and architecture are mediocre at best.

He could have felt a failure, but *I* was there to help him see that the problem was not himself but those who had what he deserved. The boy was an apt pupil! He grasped in unprecedented fullness the concept which I taught him. Instructing him deep within the hidden place of his soul, I gradually revealed to him that "unworthy others" were a barrier to his having his rightful inheritance.

Quick to receive my teaching in his inner spirit, young Schicklgruber brilliantly incarnated its implications on a global basis. Czechs, Poles, Russians, English, Gypsies, and especially the Jews held his birthright hostage! Oh, what a student! Indeed, he became a master.

He changed his name simply because he wanted another. Hitler fit him well—strong, masculine, authoritative, and Teutonic. Envy empowered him to seize a new name. Envy personified in Hitler seized countries. Envy drove his armies, fueled his political machinery, informed his propaganda, and stoked the furnaces of Dachau and Ravensbrook. What a man! What a god!

Hitler stood like the sane god he knew he was and rejected the insanity of a world that would have denied him his rightful power and glory. *I* set him free to seize, lie, manipulate, and murder. Because of me, Hitler was liberated to understand that Envy made him a god. Few have attained to his exalted freedom, soaring like an eagle above the petty, antiquated moral squeamishness that reduces gods to human beings.

Others have had bursts of brilliance: Stalin, Mao, Pol Pot, Idi Amin, Mussolini, and Alexander. But Hitler was a star in his own heaven. Those idiot sheep of the Tyrant speak of Hitler's anti-Semitism. Of course, how can the woman Israel or the child on her lap be allowed to live and usurp that which is not theirs?

The Prince and his spiritual seed spring from the woman Israel. After my rescue of Adam and Eve, the Tyrant proposed to send a seed to bruise my head and steal my rights. I taught Adam and Eve to envy with a purity and perfection that set them free. I taught Cain to envy and lifted him into the realm of the truly free. "Thou Shalt Do No Murder" lay in antique silence before the gleaming new morality of a Cain set free by Envy.

I will not—I cannot—sit still and await the blow. *I* taught Pharaoh to strangle Hebrew male infants. I was there at his elbow when Herod ordered the great slaughter in Bethlehem. Yes, it is true that Moses escaped, as did the Prince. But the efforts of Pharaoh and Herod were nonetheless among Envy's finest hours. Envy must slay the woman and her seed before they slay us.

All racial divisions, class struggles, feminist hatred, male domination, and especially religious wars are MINE. Whatever mind arises to help my cause, I am the mind behind that mind. In the deep wedges between Arabs and Jews, Serbs and Croats, Irish Catholics and their Protestant neighbors, I AM. I AM there and Envy is my virtue of choice.

The secret to divine Envy is so simple and yet so breathtakingly beautiful that I tell it with absolute delight. The key is a mantra so holy that its mere repetition turns humans into gods. It is a sacred phrase which I gave to humanity in Eden. It was the gift of fire from my mind to theirs.

In three simple words lies the essence of Envy: *"How dare they?"* That is my most insistent inner whisper. I speak it up into the gleaming corporate towers and down into the underground labyrinth of the PLO and the Ku Klux Klan. How dare they possess, know, or do that which is MINE! How dare they?

In three simple words lies the essence of Envy:
"How dare they?"

I brood over the face of the waters, restless with nauseating pockets of contentment. I am the god of the forgotten, the malcontent, the discontent, and the murmurer. The Tyrant has cast them off, a fact of which I must remind them over and over again. But I have espoused their cause. Envy, the spiritual mistress of the have-nots, is my sister.

The comedy of this is, of course, in the Tyrant's pathetic squeamishness. He is the cosmic sissy.

I was there in Solomon's throne room when two women claimed to be the mother of the same baby. I watched in frank amazement—or shall I say amusement—as Solomon called for a sword. Did he think for one moment that such dramatics could possibly intimidate a woman whose heart was soaked in pure Envy? Solomon had spent the previous night secure in his ivory palace, unaware that either woman existed.

I, and I alone, sat by the grieving woman as she watched her housemate's living baby squirming against his mother's breast. "How dare she?" I whispered, "How dare she have a living child when your child has died? How dare the Tyrant in heaven allow her child to live while yours is dead? How dare that baby suckle nourishment from any breast, so long as yours aches in loneliness?"

Yes! I was there to help her see the injustice of it all. I held the cup to her lips and braced her head ever so tenderly as she drank in Envy's sweet, sweet brew. I strengthened her heart against Solomon's theatrics. Did he think that guilt and pity could move a woman into whose bloodstream I had personally administered Envy? That woman was so far above such paltry emotions that she could not be touched by rivers of tears or oceans of baby's blood.

I hear you, Professor, asking, "But what about the innocent child?" No one can soar into such heavenly virtues as Envy while he or she hugs earthly pathos and morbid mercy. That woman understood. *No child* was innocent if her child was dead. *No mother* should be happy while she grieved. Shall mortals dance while a goddess grieves?

I remember how she wailed out her moral victory over tyrannical restraint. "Kill him! Yes, kill him!" she screamed, with Envy's fire alight in her fevered eyes. What a goddess! "Cut him in half! If I cannot have him, neither shall she!"

I shall never forget the cowardly shock in Solomon's eyes. His puny effort at so-called justice was applauded by some, to be sure, but it was a mockery. Solomon should have given the child to his rightful owner, not to his whining obsequious mother. The birth mother was willing to part *with him*. What weakness! But the goddess was willing to *part him*. That is Envy's spiritual strength! I'm disgusted by "justice" that exalts the weak and beggarly above the strong and ruthless.

The envious have-nots are not fooled by the useless pity of the haves. The kindnesses extended to the envious inflame godlike hatred. Kindness cannot kill Envy; it only fans it into a raging conflagration.

To be sure, I seldom find a goddess whose golden Envy rises to the level of infanticide. Diamonds are not valuable because of beauty only, but by virtue of rarity. Such gems are not everywhere in every generation.

But I also delight in the lesser lights along the way. A woman who would conspire to do murder because her daughter was not chosen as a high school cheerleader is not to be overlooked. The pastor who builds until his congregation is hopelessly indebted does so, to a great extent, because he envies the building and ministry of another. I am there to encourage his incipient Envy by teaching him to mouth the mantras of church growth while despising the success of his competitors. I take no small satisfaction in knowing that by helping him replace obsolete contentment with true Envy, I will spiritually access many of his people as well. I have often been able to generate a spirit of Envy strong enough to break the Tyrant's grip on an entire congregation. Such a church becomes filled with the liberated spirit of my character and active with my tactics in its staff and membership.

✖✖

You might think that I would want a sign in front that says, "Church of Lucifer." Nonsense! I want no church to bear my name.

✖✖

You might think that I would want a sign in front that says, "Church of Lucifer." Nonsense! I want no church to bear my name. Let them all bear the Tyrant's name. The character of witchcraft at work in the church with his name out front is infinitely more useful to me than a thousand warlocks or so called churches of Satan.

I have knelt at altars with a million fevered students and brought to their minds the superior spirituality of others.

It is impossible to estimate how many confused missionaries thought they were serving the Tyrant joyfully, when actually they were compelled by Envy of some relative's faith or sacrifice or devotion. What magnificent irony! Such a disturbed neurotic at work in the Tyrant's service does me more good than a thousand terrorists.

My work in this area must, of course, go largely unheralded.

Such is the nature of a god's sacrificial love. That they might know Envy's sweet delight, I humbly hide my light under a bushel. Even now I loathe to boast, but I must report the truth. I have been at work from the beginning of the great struggle.

I opened Saddam Hussein's eyes to the riches of Kuwait. How dare they possess what he did not? I beckoned revisionist historians to destroy dead heroes. How dare they be pure or honest or decent? I pump the supernatural energy of Envy straight and hot into the veins of reporters until they can see that the decent, the humble, and the honest in any discipline are affronts to their own liberated divinity and must be dragged down.

Perhaps you think I take too much on myself. No, I tell you, I was there at the bedside of King Saul. I drummed a little children's rhyme into his mind again and again until he finally burst the last debilitating bondage of the Tyrant and became a ruthless, cold, unyielding god! "Saul has slain his thousands; David his tens of thousands." How dare they!

It started as an innocent song of women and children and became the anthem of a king who became a god. Saul's envy was not only royal, but divine! Saul saw that no one, especially a sunburnt slip of a lad, had the right to one iota of praise or fame or recognition. David's youth, boldness, courage, spirituality, and innocent good looks were an outrage not to be endured.

Some have marveled at Saul's envy of such a youth. They reasoned that since Saul had the crown, he should not envy an impoverished shepherd boy. But the delightful mystery of Envy is that it defies reason. The daughter of a millionaire may envy the blonde curls of an orphan. The famous actress may envy the homey, blue-collar happiness of her childhood friend. And the home-run king with every trophy imaginable may hate the third-string catcher for his quiet confidence, his mannerly hair, or his slim hips. That is the sheer joy of Envy—it defies all circumstances, logic, and limitations.

I have helped and continue to help so many that my satisfaction is virtually boundless. I aided the unhappy boy in seducing the little girl next door, not from Lust alone, but Envy. His hate-filled Envy for her happy home life found suitable revenge in sullying her conscience.

Envy must tolerate no love, accept no loyalty, and allow no mercy, pity, or compassion to dilute its purity. Unalloyed Envy courses in the veins of the true gods. It energizes the enclosed microcosms of society with divine fire. Officers' clubs, dugouts, studio lots, and faculty lounges blaze with Envy. It disallows all relationships. Envy alone finds the godlike fury to weep at the rejoicing of others and rejoice at their tears.

Because of the corruption of the Tyrant, I cannot often speak openly of Envy's majestic sweetness. Some people must start with lowly cousins, like competition, and move gradually toward Envy. At first, most begin in a competitive desire to do better than others. But ultimately, many will graduate to an infinitely superior desire to see others do worse.

I have been there from the first, teaching, helping, and assisting the sons and daughters of Adam to envy. I helped Eve to envy the Tyrant, Cain to envy Abel, and Hitler to envy the Jews.

I stood in the desert camps of the Hebrews and whispered questions into Miriam's ear. "Is Moses the only one who hears from heaven? Wasn't he living in Egypt's luxury while you languished in a slave hovel? And what about all those years while Moses made a family in Midian? Did he understand the mystique of maidenhood or feminine intuition fashioned at the cost of unrequited love?"

At first she had to be helped to see the unfairness of it. She had to feel indignant at the woman of Cush whom her brother had married. She had to see that the Tyrant was treacherous in his favoritism to Moses. "Is a prophet better than a prophetess? A priest than a priestess? Who made this rule? How dare they!"

Once she asked that, the way was open before her to ascend to pure goddess Envy. She could see Moses' evil motives. She could see what no one else could see—the monstrous wickedness of a Tyrant who would grant her brother the spiritual leadership, prerogatives, and prestige that by all rights should have been *hers*. Why, it was an evil conspiracy to deny Miriam her rights.

Her eyes at last were opened. The spirit of her mother Eve stirred in her inner soul. The virgin Miriam, desert goddess, holy mother of Envy. And the virgin conceived and brought forth—Me.

CHAPTER FIVE

෧෪

Michael Answers Concerning Envy

"Professor, are you able to keep up?" Michael asked me.

"Yes, I think so," I answered, surprised to be so suddenly drawn into the conversation.

"Do you need a rest?"

"I seem to be fine."

"Get on with it!" Lucifer yelled.

Michael fixed Lucifer with a steady gaze and said softly, yet in a tone that crackled with electricity, "Silence, serpent! This human must not be damaged. That was the rule."

To this Lucifer only muttered unintelligibly and sat on the back of my couch with his feet on the cushions. Michael watched him retreat, then turned back to me.

෧෪

You see, Professor, Lucifer twists everything. He is a counterfeit himself and the father of all counterfeiters. For every Mary he desires a Miriam, and for every gift of God he fashions a bogus currency. Even from the first, even in Eden, that serpent hated Adam's rest.

Heaven's joy was absolute in Adam's contented bliss. Eve's happiness was God's delight. Indeed, all the angels in heaven rejoiced in their undiluted peace. What could ever disturb their calm and tranquil Garden?

Adam and Eve, unshackled, unblemished, and unburdened, strolled hand in hand beneath the shade trees. They knew nothing of shame or fear or bloodshed. Disease was unknown and distress undiscovered. Open, naked, innocent, and utterly delightful, they had yet to tremble under the tyranny of lust and greed. The horror of bondage and the cosmic criminality of sin was not yet. Ah! I sigh at the very memory of the beauty of their Edenic paradise.

Then the long, evil nightmare of the human soul began. At first, I did not comprehend the damage that had been done. Then I saw Adam's eyes and shivered, for death was in his eyes. He looked back over his shoulder at the closed Garden, and death was in his eyes. He stared ahead at the wretched world of toil and fear which lay before him, and death was in his eyes. He looked at the woman from whose tender hand he had accepted the fruit, and his own death was mirrored in her eyes.

Adam's sin made the living into the dead. Lucifer unleashed evil. Adam unleashed extinction.

Rivaled only by Lucifer's tragic destruction, Adam's fall marred a visage previously untouched by aught but the hand of God. Lucifer's rebellion made angels into demons. Adam's sin made the living into the dead. Lucifer unleashed evil. Adam unleashed extinction.

Of course, the problem is that humanity has no memory of its life in Eden. When death becomes normal, life seems dreamlike, faraway, and unrealistic. The real tragedy is not the death of humanity, but that humanity embraced its own death. Owning death, Adam's race became dead in its death.

The sons of Adam cannot imagine what a ghoulish imitation of life they present to the angels who remember Adam. To angels, the race of Adam is seen over against a memory which humanity itself has lost. We cannot help but regard them as the weak and beggarly ghosts of an Adam so vibrant, so alive, so—how can I say it?—so mighty! Yes, that's it—*mighty!*

Adam had the power to subdue. His fallen children could only surrender. Adam had authority to multiply. His offspring could merely procreate. Ah, this account is wasted. I can sense it. Why do I go on about it, when the sons and daughters of Adam and Eve weep no more for their own lost estate? *That* is the autobiography of Lucifer. He is the author and finisher of death. He is the destruction and the confusion of man and the doorway of the grave.

✖✖

Lucifer's monstrous pride birthed the hellish Envy of a humanity ensnared in a conspiracy of death.

✖✖

Lucifer's malevolent pride envied Adam's birthright. He plotted and schemed the death of man. Denying the authority of God, his Creator, Lucifer rebelled in self-destructive arrogance. Hurled from heaven by the hand of God, Lucifer determined to attack the pearl of heaven's handiwork.

The dragon lashes with his tail, breathing fire and opening wide his jaws to devour the woman and her seed. Lucifer hates even the tiniest trace elements of Eden that still glitter in the race like flecks of gold in a muddy riverbank.

Lucifer's monstrous pride birthed the hellish Envy of a humanity ensnared in a conspiracy of death. Confederate with the grave and spurred on by Lucifer and his demons, Envy made Adam's children ugly, mean, and ruthless.

The angels are astonished, nay horrified, as they watch the shrinking and shriveling of human souls pickled in the brine of comparison. We watch from the windows of heaven in shocked amazement at humanity's relentless, driven quest for recognition, fame, and glory. They grow less and less, losing all hope of happiness. Nothing is ever enough. Contentment, joy, and relationships are destroyed. Adam and Eve can no longer enjoy together the beauty of a butterfly. They are isolated by their envious suspicion. Does he know something she doesn't? Does he think he is better because he is a male? Is she trying to take his place?

Their Envy is often born of nothing more than broad thinking: "That person got the job I wanted because he is *better* than I am" creates an inevitable posture of Envy. The more narrowed version: "That person got the job because he works harder than I" allows for healthier latitude, differences of gifts, and more wholesome appreciation of goals and expenditure.

It often appears to angels that people possessed by Envy will go to any length to reduce the perceived gap between themselves and the object of their envy. What pitiable folly! They spend themselves into bankruptcy, put themselves recklessly in harm's way, and drive themselves to despair in their futile efforts to prove that they are as rich, brave, or successful as another.

When they cannot escape their envy with their own success, they dream and scheme the failure of the other. The incessant faultfinding and the murderous gossip campaigns are Envy's fruit. The person, at first admired, must finally be reduced to rubble, once Envy mixes with admiration.

Envy is not, as many believe, the simple desire to have what another has. It is the hatred of what another has, or of what another is. Envy is not a longing for more than I have. That is a sin, to be sure, but it is not Envy. Envy is the longing for another not to have. Envy is more about depriving than gaining.

A wealthy farmer and a poverty-ridden peasant live near one

another. One might easily surmise that the peasant envies the rich man. And indeed the peasant may envy his neighbor's wealth, his comforts, his pleasure and his leisure with all the hatred and spite and malice of his burdened soul. That is not difficult to predict. But from there, the path of Envy is thorny and crooked. Its turns and twists are unapparent in the fog of human misconception.

✵

Envy is not, as many believe, the simple desire to have what another has. It is the hatred of what another has, or of what another is.

✵

We may assume the envious peasant will turn to angry socialism. Indeed, communism is fueled by frustrated Envy. Communism thrives on the inability to stand the sight of another's prosperity. Socialism first admits, then idolizes, then legitimizes, and finally legislates Envy.

What Westerners exulting in the "death of communism" may not so readily see is that the consummate capitalist may well be fueled not by the greed he denies, nor by the competition to which he admits, but by the Envy to which he is oblivious.

The peasant dreams of revolution. The corporate raider dreams of the bankruptcy of his competitor, and believes that his is a healthy, robust Western capitalism. But his energy derives from a vicious, venal fantasy of the financial destruction of a fellowman. He squirms a bit at the mention of Greed as it falls from his pastor's lips, but not at all at the word Envy.

Envy, however, is his even more than the peasant's. This particular capitalist has seen a certain competitor's life, his dignity perhaps, his reputation in the field, or nothing more than his bearing or the way his employees admire him. At a party a word of admiration was spoken, or perhaps an article in a trade journal extolled the competitor's virtue. Whatever the cause, however it sneaked in, Envy has taken root.

He does not *want* anything. He is not greedy for a luxury automobile. At least, it is not Greed that grips him now. It is not *wanting* but *hating* that drives him to plot his competitor's ruin. He knows in his deepest heart that he cannot *have* the virtues or admiration or standing in the community of this envied one. If he *wants* anything, it is that his envied enemy high up there above him be brought low. He does not want to have; he *wants* his adversary *not* to have.

His Envy has made the desire of his heart entirely other-destructive. He dreams of financial murder. He fantasizes about gloating over news accounts that report his enemy's disastrous end. He tingles with anticipation at the thought of his proud, widely admired enemy wallowing in shame, defeat, or perhaps even scandal.

The Bolshevik revolutionary coldly put a bullet through the head of the Czar. French peasants mocked and laughed as pleading aristocrats were dragged to the guillotine. Yet they did not have any real expectation of *being* czars or aristocrats, or of living in palaces. Their Envy has not lifted them to possess the gates of their enemies. Instead, it has shrunk them to become lethal dwarfs who cannot climb up, and will poison the upward path for those above them. The self-righteous capitalist who sees them as radicals and anarchists cannot see himself as also a child of Satan.

To the angels, of course, the face of Envy clearly bears the stamp of Lucifer. As he envied God, so people envy one another. The worst kind of all is that spiritual Envy within the church that drapes itself in religion. We behold it in horror.

An associate minister at a certain church, against policy, borrows money from church members and then fails to repay it. The senior pastor, whom he admires a great deal, discovers it and confronts him. The younger man is offered an opportunity to quietly resign and leave without scandal. Outwardly, the associate seems grateful and appears to accept the gracious offer with humility and repentance.

Inwardly, however, the young man seethes with rage. He quietly sets about to destroy his senior pastor's reputation with a carefully calculated campaign of subtlety and gossip. Unwilling to ascribe sin to his beloved associate, the senior pastor plunges on, confused at the rising tide of unexplainable opposition, turmoil, and energized factionalism in his congregation. Friends and advisors tell him of the associate's disloyalty and insubordination, but he won't believe the truth. He stands by his associate, still willing to show grace.

The pastor's magnanimous trust of him and continuing patience do not shame the youthful lieutenant. Rather, his campaign of spite grows more vengeful. The associate's wife keeps the phone lines hot with stirring strife. Finally the volcano erupts into open fratricide; the method of evil, the deadly sin that lay at the bottom of it all, was Envy.

Exactly when would be difficult even for the angels to tell, but at some point Satan entered and admiration became Envy. Envy would destroy its object, itself, and all in its path. Envy is the mother of a thousand sins in the church. Lying, deceit, and disloyalty lie at its door. And Satan is within.

A rock musician is murdered by an envious "fan" because in death the star is no threat to the talentless and the mediocre. The junior staff member leads an insidious rebellion against the successful senior pastor whom he has admired exceedingly. Why? Because in the associate's heart, in some horrible moment, the strychnine of Envy laced admiration with death. His mutinous schism is not merely an effort to have, but to deprive. Stripped of some of his glory, defeated and despoiled, the senior pastor looks a bit less anointed. Not quite as *enviable*.

Comedians, movie critics, and political pundits are the

commissioned agents of the envious. "Go and drag our heroes down for us, down where we can get at them. Splatter them with mud, bloody them, mock them—anything—but get them down here with us. Tell us that Shakespeare did not write his plays, that Michelangelo was homosexual, and that Jefferson owned slaves. Tell us again and again of their mistakes and foibles. Remind us of faults both real and imagined. Their lofty gifts and graces are more than we can bear! How dare they be what we are not? How dare they be talented, beautiful, rich, or even righteous? Most of all, righteous!"

Daniel proved more righteous than Nebuchadnezzar's other advisors. Indeed, his adversaries admitted to his righteousness. They agreed that he would never be found breaking decent laws. But his decency did not inspire them to be more decent. It merely fueled their envious conspiracy to pass an indecent law.

Envy kills all love, pity, mercy, and compassion.

In Envy indecent men used an indecent law to bring down a man whom they knew and agreed among themselves to be more righteous than they.

Envy reserves no room for loyalty. Absalom's loyalty to his father, David, was disallowed by his Envy. The self-destructiveness of Envy is incredible. Hanging from a tree limb at the point of his own death, Absalom undoubtedly comforted himself with the knowledge that, though he was about to die, the lustre on David's crown would never again gleam as brightly.

Envy kills all love, pity, mercy, and compassion. Envy hears evil in an apology and sees murderous deceit behind every act of kindness. Envy drapes itself around righteous indignation and ascribes evil motives to its object. Miriam's outrage at Moses' marriage to the Cushite woman was a subterfuge. Her legalistic indignation camouflaged her Envy. She first admired, then envied her brother's spirituality, holiness, and religious preeminence. She envied his relationship with God. In her singleness, she perversely envied his spouse. She envied his maleness, his meekness, and his marriage.

So it is in all of life. Those who are single envy the intimacy of the married. The married envy the liberty of the unmarried. The prosaic and provincial envy their celebrities, then pay talk-show hosts to expose the shame and weaknesses of the enviable rich and famous. Having knocked over the straw "heroes" of AIDS-infected movie stars, the petty and puny little people leering into their TVs cackle and gloat at the fall of yet another who made them feel less good about themselves.

In the art world, Envy corrupts beauty no less than virtue. Envy steadfastly refuses to accept the rules of life—order, balance, and beauty. Envy knows that such rules define the grand talent of true art. They also define mediocrity. Envy puts the grappling hooks to true greatness by elevating its opposite. Envy says, "If I cannot create great symphonies, I will create cacophony and call it melody, disorder and call it balance, ugliness and call it beauty." Envy indulges in the idolatry of its own failure. Envy is the root of the lethal hatred the mediocre feel for great, and the near-famous feel for the famous, and the religious for the righteous.

Worst of all, of course, is what Envy does to the envious. Because it disallows authentic relationships, while at the same time requiring utterly unrealistic and unattainable goals, Envy isolates absolutely. The result is utter alienation.

Envy consumes the daughters of Eve. It drives them toward a wombless, breastless obsession with what they are not, rather than who they are. The sons of Adam wander like haunted shades in waterless wastelands, obsessively fearful that another may find the oasis before they do. Without happiness, they settle for heart-less glee when they discover in the desert sand the dried bones of competitors.

Alienated from each other in paranoid fear, they cannot see the lonely monsters they have become. Envious of one another, they fight to the death for scraps. In Envy of God, they miss their redemption. Envy dances round the foot of the cross and weeps at the resurrection.

Dialogue III:

Lucifer: I must laugh to keep from going insane.

Michael: How droll! Wholesome laughter is indeed a hedge against insanity. But your laughter is evil and you are already insane. You can manage only mocking laughter because your madness has no defense against the sanity of truth.

Lucifer: Now you do make me laugh. You call this drivel about envy *truth?* You are but a puppet of the Tyrant and his Princeling. You would turn such a great virtue into a "straw sin," then burn it down to convince weak-minded mortals.

Michael: Envy is no straw sin. It is...

Lucifer: The very stuff that sets us free from Tyranny. Without Envy I would still be as you are.

Michael: Would to God you were as I am!

Lucifer: I am as I am. I was a puppet-angel. Now, I am god. That's Envy's work. From subservient angel to self-made god! Only Envy stirred me to rebel and finally flee the velvet nest of my imprisonment.

Michael: Careful, Lucifer! You verge on truth. Except for the rhetorical revisionism, you are careening dangerously close to actual truth. It was indeed Envy that cost you heaven. The Prince taught His disciples to pray the opposite of Envy.

"Thy kingdom come. Thy will be done."

That is the prayer that keeps them in His kingdom. You lost it by claiming your own will *and* kingdom.

Lucifer: Agggh! That dirty little ditty melts gods like candle wax. *Thy* kingdom? *Thy* will? You bovine creatures nauseate me. Why must it be *his* kingdom? Why *his* will? Can't you think for yourselves? Don't you have a will? Don't you want a kingdom?

Michael: You claimed your will and your kingdom and lost all. It is always so with all who do.

Lucifer: I lost nothing! I fled! I escaped the bully to whom you submit. But even if it were as you say, that's just my point. If only the Tyrant can will or rule or have or even claim a kingdom, then all others are nothing but his servants.

Michael: What, again? Twice to be so very near to the truth? Yes! The King's servant is he who submits to His will. Who knows and obeys His will inherits His kingdom.

Lucifer: A slave in a kingdom is still a slave.

Michael: A child in a kingdom is free. An archangel in chains in a pit is a slave forever.

Lucifer: You always resort to threats.

Michael: Never! Promises.

Lucifer: Your smug remarks are typical.

Michael: The envious who see contentment as resignation, make the quiet confidence of heaven into smug superiority.

Lucifer: I am your equal!

Michael: Certainly. We are both nothing.

Lucifer: Don't you want anything?

Michael: I want for nothing, and I have all I want if I want His will.

Lucifer: You will never own anything.

Michael: Never.

Lucifer: You will never speak as a god, calling your will into reality!

Michael: Never.

Lucifer: You will never be a god!

Michael: Never!

Lucifer: Well, we settled *that!*

Michael: *That* was settled from forever—for both of us.

Lucifer: You infuriate me.

Michael: Don't be absurd. Fury is in your wings. You are the wrathful angel of terror.

Lucifer: What a delicious word *terror* is.

Michael: *Wrath* is next on the list, I suppose.

Lucifer: I am warming to this.

Michael: Interesting choice of words.

Lucifer: Shut up.

CHAPTER SIX

Lucifer on Wrath

I am the god of the terrorist. The egotism of the Tyrant knows no boundary. He allows no terror but his own. He and his brood speak constantly of *his* wrath but make no allowances for humanity. I see every man a god, and every god a terrorist.

Why, even in his wrath, the Tyrant speaks of mercy! What gutless corruption! Can he not even be pure in wrath? He speaks of grace. What putrid nonsense. He sickens me in his weakness.

The wrath of godlike terrorism is utterly inconsolable. It is cold, steely, and intractable. It bears no appeal. Wrath resents "more information" as arrogant rebellion, and all further discussion as intolerable insolence. A willingness to be entreated is unendurable. Wrath prohibits forgiveness, denies compassion, and disallows any trace of mercy. Wrath will *not* listen to reason.

Wrath is pride in action. It sweeps away all obstacles to SELF. What stands in the way of appetite, satisfaction, or self-exaltation must be executed! The Wrath of gods could be called a sin only by a sick and perverted Tyrant.

I must help the sons and daughters of Adam to cast off their sheepish self-denial and rise from the ashes of impotence to a new life of wrathful power. Even a little mouse like you, Professor, can be taught to roar. I must vigilantly stand at the elbow of the uncontrolled and uncontrollable. I must stoke the inner furnace which melts the wrath of frustration until the molten flow of godlike rage rains lethal lava down upon the cowed heads of authority figures, parents, and chums. Imminent eruption must constantly terrorize all that lies in the path of the wrathful.

When everything and everyone around him lives in constant fear of his violent explosions, an ordinary teenage boy becomes a god indeed. He rules as lord in his parents' home. The subterranean rage lurking unseen and unnamed in the core of his being reigns supreme over adults three times his age. What a god! What a god!

From a distance of three thousand meters, the hidden sniper decides who dies. He sits in godlike and unapproachable judgment. From behind the cold steel barrel of his rifle, he dispenses terror with remorseless, methodical precision. The IRA bomber drives down the streets of London or Belfast in the merciless knowledge that he is god. The very thought of him gives children nightmares. He runs his hand over a box of plastic explosives and Wrath like a river of hate swirls around his soul in black, remorseless death. What a god!

I must help husbands and fathers to see the godlike power of verbal terrorism. The husband who stalks his own wife, waiting, sniping with his words, is likewise a terrorist god. Year after year he and I must work to terrorize her soul. We waste her joy with savage impenitent glee. We plant the plastic explosives of his inconsolable and unpredictable rage so as to steal her morale, kill her nerves, and destroy her resistance. For years, she turns her baleful eyes to him for mercy. Idiot! Mercy? From a terrorist? From a god? Earth forbid.

When mercy never comes, she, at last, seeks for refuge, appeasement, anything to stop the bombing. The campaign of terror must increase, not decrease. Bombs must go off in her face at moments well-timed for maximum effect. Her soul must be pummeled by a bombardment so relentless, so at random and without escape, that at last, she crumples under the knowledge that her husband is a god. He need never raise a fist. His verbal terror makes her a panic-stricken refugee with no place to hide. Her defeat is his deification. Their children's battered souls and wounded spirits lie before his throne like trophies of conquest. The Wrath of a god devours them daily. They are slain by the breath of his nostrils. Divine in his Wrath, he is feared by them. His Wrath becomes the central fact of their pitiful lives.

Now the Tyrant would make of him a merciful, loving, benevolent little image of himself. The Tyrant would deny him his right to dominate utterly. The Tyrant would crush his godly pride with prosaic preachments about "the restraint of common morality." But I make him a god whose life is lived above the tree line of such a weakling mentality.

❧❧

The modern verbal terrorist of suburbia who lacerates his wife and children until they live in stark, undiminished fear of his explosions is brother to the IRA bomber, and the cold-eyed assassin.

❧❧

The IRA terrorist trembles not for innocent children blown to pieces by his well-placed bombs. Their mangled little bodies are the awful proof of his divine Wrath. The unreasonable insanity of his Wrath is its very power. To the astonished onlooker, it makes no sense. Hence, its terror is heightened all the more.

The terrorist lurking behind his anonymity is like ME. Silent, relentless, merciless, he strikes in the random and unpredictable horror of a true god. He cannot even be found. The modern verbal terrorist of suburbia who lacerates his wife and children until they live in stark, undiminished fear of his explosions is brother to the IRA bomber, and the cold-eyed assassin. They are all brothers and gods and I am the father-god of them all.

The common human being will more easily scale the heights of Wrath than you may think. The "leap" from the average childhood temper tantrum to an ax murder is no leap at all. It is rather an easy trail of tiny half-steps. The breadcrumbs of revenge lead the tempestuous child up the slope to the peak of divine Wrath.

Of course, I must help. I must be there to point out the wound. I must enlighten as to the *extent* of the wound. It must become a fixation, a devouring angry faucet that drips acid without ceasing.

I had to help Saul see the conspiracy hatched between the rebel David and his own disloyal son, Jonathan. That conspiracy had to become more real to Saul than Jonathan's love or David's protestations of innocence. Soon it throbbed in Saul's temples. It coursed hotly through his veins and haunted his every dream. Just the sight of David's empty chair brought the conspiracy to his mind. Saul finally came to understand that Jonathan's soothing words were a cover-up and that guileless eyes hid a thousand disloyalties.

When the volcano of Saul's rage finally erupted, it was not merely the hot ash of kingly displeasure. Saul was a god in his Wrath. To hurl a javelin at his own son? A god, I tell you! A god, indeed! That kind of Wrath is real.

When Cain's wrath erupted and he slew his sibling, Abel, I was in his eyes and upon his countenance. When Nebuchadnezzar ordered the Hebrew rebels into the fiery furnace, my face lay upon his.

Jonathan dodged the spear and searched his father's familiar eyes for reassurance and comfort. He hoped for some trace of tender love and remorse. But by then, Saul was a god. I was dark and fearsome upon the brow of King Saul. It was my light that Jonathan saw in his father's eyes.

To be sure, I must constantly assist all the children of Adam. I made Adam what he became. I made Herod and Pharaoh and Hitler, and I am not by the eons weakened in my resolve. I helped Cain to see the exquisite, godlike delight of Wrath released. I, and I alone, helped Cain to know the joy of breaking that last pitiful bond of moral restraint that stands between the sons of Adam and their destiny.

"What did Abel do?" you may ask. The very question betrays how confused you humans are. That is utterly irrelevant. Abel did not *do* anything. The *fact* of him, of his obsequious subservience to the Tyrant, of the Tyrant's blatant favoritism, and the fact that Abel was gallantly confident and calm in his claim to spiritual superiority, were more than enough.

I know you humans will ask, "Did Abel deserve to die?" When you ask questions like that, I grow weary. It was not that Abel deserved to die. It was that Cain deserved to kill. Cain knew that a god dare not suffer the outrage of Wrath checked by statute or convention. The naked fact of the grievance, not some objective analysis of its level, is fundamental to true liberty. I must teach Cain's children in every generation what their father knew. If their anger is justified, it must respect no bounds. The only rational, temperate response of a god to anger felt is anger expressed, and that god himself is the only conceivable party to moderate its expression in the least. The appropriate expression of anger is what the god deems to be appropriate. That is the Wrath of god.

The college co-ed who sends a man to jail for a date rape he did not commit is the goddess of rape. She has punctured his life with her accusation. The jilted girl who stabs her ex-boyfriend's current lover with a pair of scissors is a goddess.

The teenage girl who, when corrected, rains curses on her mother's head, does not yet fully realize she is a goddess, but she is sister to the murderer and the false accuser. As the young woman's screams of "I hate you!" pierce the air, her mother cowers before her much as the naked women prisoners at Dachau and Ravensbrook trembled before the truncheons of their female guards. She does not yet think she belongs to such exalted company. She believes her tantrum to be but the childish desire to "have her way," but she is too modest. It doth not yet appear what she shall be, but when the need arises, she shall be like ME.

She will learn to channel her wrath without diluting it. She will finally graduate from screams and tantrums to false accusations. She will learn the art of the trembling lip and steady but dewy eyes that make for a "credible witness." She will bring down her prey like the goddess Diana. The outraged language of strident feminism will be the bow in her hand and the emotionally charged rhetoric of sexual harassment her arrows. Former mentors, bosses, and colleagues will tremble before her. Let them. She will be a goddess by then, a terrorist queen of the night, who can destroy in her wrath all who dare to resist her.

Potiphar's wife was a goddess. She ran to her husband with Joseph's coat in hand and bitter tears upon her cheek. What a woman! A veritable queen of terror! Let Joseph languish in prison. He deserves it. After all, who does he think he is?

Jezebel took Naboth's life and vineyard. Salome took John the Baptist's head. What goddesses! Their Pride led to Envy and Envy to Wrath. And what Wrath! Their murderous plots, schemes, and false accusations were their genius, and their mercilessness was the proof of their divinity. Nothing could stand before them. They scorched the earth and left corpses behind them. They were not just women; they were armies with banners unfurled.

Though I may not see the like of Jezebel again, I am not altogether without hope. Given the right weapons, many women are capable of becoming goddesses of terror. The key to their self-actualization as goddesses is to understand the fundamental truth

of "justified rage." Mere mortals link the grievousness of the outrage to the response. Such puny moral logic allows inherent limitations which are not fitting for a god or goddess.

In other words, when the wrathful see that justifiable anger
permits any responsive action, they stretch toward the divine. But
when they think in terms of "appropriate reaction," they shrink
away from the gigantic to the moral dwarfism that dominates the
Tyrant's brood of worms.

A man who shouts at his wife because she first shouted at him
is a moral pygmy. He is trapped on her plane and she dictates the
terms. But when he responds to her shout by hitting her or even
killing her, he has stated in no uncertain terms that he is her god.

He *must* state the terms. His actions must be based on the *justice of his wounding,* not on its severity. She pouts, he hits. She
hits, he murders. She insults, he rapes. She denies his advances, he
hacks her into pieces and incinerates her dismembered corpse.
That is the Wrath of a god.

The child who murders his parents because they denied him a
car is a giant of Wrath. He is a god, not merely because he had
the moral strength to remove an obstacle to his will, but because
he refused to "control himself," "measure his response," or
"react appropriately." He is a god who has declared himself above
the frontiers which limit the Wrath of mortals. Any petulant brat
may sulk at having his will frustrated. Though certainly better
than mute acquiescence, sulking is hardly the Wrath of a god.
The explosion, the magnificent eruption that smashes furniture,
breaks china or threatens a murder-suicide—*that* is Wrath. Only
that can teach his miserable, sniveling parents that they have no
authority over him and that his Wrath will be unrestricted.

As they stare at him in horrified silence, they ask, "Did we give
birth to this god?" Well they might ask. Flesh gives birth to flesh.
But the spirit of the child-god is from ME. He was once theirs in
the flesh. But now, as his splendid Wrath devours their shriveled

souls, they know the awesome truth. He has sliced away the umbilical cord of natural birth to be born again of new spirit. He is now a god. The knowledge of it in their eyes is his supreme delight, his coronation and glory. A god, at last. A god of Wrath.

Imagine a young woman who works for an older man. She admires and respects him. She even begins to develop incipient romantic feelings for her icon. That is important, for those feelings, finding no response in her "boss cum father cum idol," will fester into a painful lesion that oozes rejection, resentment, and bitterness.

Still, she is not quite ready to make the great leap toward divinity. The recipe of Wrath bubbling in the caldron still wants a few key ingredients. Frustration in her own professional life is "wing of bat." Embarrassing inability to relate to men is "eye of newt." *Now* double, double, toil and trouble!

The object of her idolatry enjoys promotion after promotion. His success separates him from her abiding mediocrity. Her divine virtues finally rise like cream to the top. Pride and envy replace affection and admiration. Now she lacks only opportunity for her goddess self to rise in majestic, outraged, Wrath.

Then it happens! The moment she has waited for. He is appointed to a nationally important position. The goddess-terrorist strikes! Her accusations of impropriety cannot be defended, for there are no witnesses. Like a calloused sniper she deals cold death with ferocious accuracy. She has broken the old moral bondage which binds the daughters of Eve to a repugnant mortality and denies them their goddess RIGHTS! She lies convincingly, weeps pathetically, and hides behind a veil of respectability. She does not rant and rave. Her accusations are not squandered stupidly in wild broad strokes. Far from it. A terrorist bomber who parks his explosive-laden truck in a shopping district does not rage and scream. He walks away in the cold, indomitable Wrath of a polar god. Even so, from her assumed perch of high moral superiority, she sits before the news cameras smiling in frigid Wrath. Death is in her eyes.

✠✠✠

Wrath behaves any way it wants,
demands its own way,
is easily provoked,
and sees evil in all others.

✠✠✠

O holy Wrath that knows no antique moral fence. O Wrath of the goddess, Salome, before whose feet the headless body of John the Baptist lies. Now she is a goddess. Her Wrath is neither measured nor "appropriate." It is poured out upon her victim's head in full fury. His pathetic eyes are full of shock and hurt and confusion. The fool! He cannot see. He doesn't even understand. She is a goddess. Her Wrath is justified. This is my daughter in whom I am well pleased.

Though I speak with the pride of a peacock or with demonic power and have not Wrath, I am a paper god. And though I have the gift of persuasion and can manipulate others spiritually and emotionally, and though I claim miraculous powers which I do not have, so that others envy me and have not Wrath, I am nothing.

Though I gain the world while tricking others into believing a lie and have not Wrath, it profiteth my flesh little.

Wrath is impatient, mocks kindness, envies with a passion, vaunts itself, and is full of pride.

Wrath behaves any way it wants, demands its own way, is easily provoked, and sees evil in all others. Wrath rejoices in iniquity, but despises what weaklings call truth. Wrath will not wait; it demands instant gratification. Wrath respects no limits; truth can be slaughtered and spiritual gifts can be defamed, the Bible can be burned, and men made into mortals. For mortals know only in part, but as a god, the partial is hateful to me indeed. When I was a mortal, I spoke as a mortal. But when I became a god, I spoke as a god. For mortals are humble and meek before the Tyrant. And now abideth these three—Pride, Envy, and Wrath. But a god without Wrath is hardly a god.

CHAPTER SEVEN

Michael Answers Concerning Wrath

I tell you, Professor, it is heartbreaking to see what has become of you humans. Adam was a giant in Eden, and Eve a queen of grace and beauty. Adam strode through the Garden, assured and confident in the quiet authority of a plenipotentiary. God named the night and the day, for time comes from the palm of the eternal. Adam had no authority over sun and moon or the rising tide. God named Adam, for Adam is the creature of God. That truth is hated by Lucifer above all things.

But Adam named the rest—wife, children, beasts of the field. He named them, loved them, knew them, and cared for them as fellow inhabitants of the ordered paradise of God. They enjoyed his stewardship and prospered in undiminished wholeness. Adam was a generous, loving, kind, and tender colossus of strength and virtue. The birds lovingly sang him to sleep, and his wife had no fear of his strength. That he who was her comfort, protection, and delight should ever be fearsome or loathsome to her was utterly unthinkable. Adam was a giant before Wrath entered his heart by Lucifer.

What irony that Lucifer's lies of independence should make Adam and Eve slaves. Lucifer, you ancient pimp, you have had your turn with Wrath. Be silent. You pander to pride for the corruption of giants. You sell lies about love and deliver only brutality and rape. You drag down and destroy. You bring confusion out of order, and chaos is your handiwork.

Lucifer, you remember. Oh, yes, Professor, look at him. That is what drives him on. That memory of what Adam was remains fresh in Lucifer's mind and haunts his demon spirits. It is the memory of Adam, very nearly as much as his hatred of God, which compels the Prince of Darkness up and down the avenues of men. Lucifer cannot elude the memory of Adam's majesty. He cannot outrun it. It haunts him, terrorizes him, and looms before his eyes. In that one way Lucifer is like God—he remembers Adam as he was.

Every time a baby kicks and screams its way into life, Lucifer howls his futile rage against the coming of the day.

Lucifer remembers the terrible beauty of Adam's countenance in the morning sun. Lucifer can still see him standing there in the Garden of God with a visage unmarred by sin. Lucifer knows that Adam was made to reign. The seed of the woman is the one great horror of Lucifer.

With a hammer in his hand and the stinking sweat of fear on his brow, Lucifer pounds away in driven desperation at the face of God's paramount creation. Reigning blows like thunderbolts upon the brow of Adam's kin, Lucifer rages out the foaming Wrath of his own frustration.

From Eden, Lucifer's hopes of obliterating God from the face of Adam have obsessed him and his hosts. Every time a baby kicks and screams its way into life, Lucifer howls his futile rage against the coming of the day. He looks into the miserable hut of an Indian untouchable in the putrid back alleys of Calcutta and sees a suckling baby put to his mother's breast. Despite the grim poverty and the stench and the apparent helplessness of the little creature, Lucifer sees the image of God among the filth. And he trembles.

Lucifer must pull the child down. He must erase from his form and face the likeness of his Creator's glory. Lucifer knows he must unleash *upon* the child a storm of evil. And he must unleash *within* the child a deluge of sin. Lucifer wants a son, and he is impotent. He wants to create, and all that he can manage is to steal, kill, and destroy.

The proud, envious Wrath of heaven wasted consumes Lucifer. Just as he pumps his own furious, inconsolable grief into the veins of Adam's sons and daughters, Lucifer's futile rage put the stone in Cain's hand and loaded the Nazi rifles in the Warsaw ghetto.

The angels are astonished at the pervasiveness of Wrath in modern society. Not since the days of Noah have violence and rapine so filled the cities of men. Abused children and women weep in terror when their fathers and husbands stumble home with drunken Wrath dark upon their faces. Aroused by frustrations birthed in Lust and Greed and all the other deadly sins, the Wrath of men has fashioned a deadly society in Lucifer's image.

What really frightens the angels, of course, is the weak acquiescence with which humanity endures poisonous Wrath. When people look in the mirror, can't they see how, in Wrath, they resemble Lucifer? To the angels it seems most terrifying that demonic Wrath seethes just under the epidermal robes and rituals of the church, no less than in the bars and brothels. We see explosive Wrath demolish churches and families, and we wonder at the presumption of saints who carry Wrath's deadly acid so carelessly bound up in their own garments. Do they not know that with every step Wrath threatens to slash out and burn both themselves and those around them? How can they fail to see how it disfigures them?

We angels stare in frank and undiluted horror when the very children of God foam out their Wrath upon one another until their faces and limbs are scarred beyond recognition. Let some announcement be made from the pulpit or some change in church policy be published with which they disagree and the acid flows. It burns and sears until behind it remains only monstrous masks of scarred deformity where the perfect complexion of a sweet, unblemished bride should glorify her King.

Wrath is, in part, a twisted tactic of violence designed to control, limit, motivate, or intimidate.

Wrath loses all sense of dimension. It makes huge issues of the insignificant and opens irreparable wounds over minor disagreements. Wrath sees plots and conspiracies where they do not exist, hears unbearable insults where none were intended, and perceives dire threats and ultimatums in the most ordinary of objections.

Wrath is energized by fear. It reasons, "If I do not act or react radically, I may be considered weak. It may happen again, and I will not be in control." Therefore, it explodes. Wrath is, in part, a twisted tactic of violence designed to control, limit, motivate, or intimidate. That has always been Lucifer's modus operandi.

Of course, no sin can become bondage unless it is reinforced with pleasure. There is no such thing as evil for its own sake. Not even Lucifer himself is wicked without motive. Lucifer is not pure in his evil, in the same way that God is perfect in His holiness. God is holy without motivation. He is "I AM" holy. Lucifer's evil is motivated by self-interest and, therefore, is not simply evil for its own sake.

The same thing is true of those under Lucifer's hand. He knows that they will not do evil just because it is evil. Their sin must be reinforced again and again with the steel cables of pleasure. Sin that gives no pleasure will not be repeated frequently enough to become bondage. Lucifer will not withdraw the pleasure until the bondage is, barring a miracle of grace, fixed forever.

Humans in bondage cannot see themselves as they are. Angels turn their faces away, for we cannot bear the sight. Humans in bondage grow so insensitive to the spiritual realm that they cannot even see the chains which they drag. They go about like warped ghosts in whom life grows gradually dimmer. How pathetic to see them wasted and fading, and to know that they think themselves whole, free, and fully alive.

That which locks the chains in place is pleasure. There must be some reward or the sin will not comprehend the light. Only self-gratification will sink the steel rods and bars into their flesh and squeeze their souls into prisoners as lifeless as walking ghosts.

The "pleasure" of Wrath is the exquisite anticipation of inflicting punishment. The actual eruption of Wrath is but its release. The final violent explosion is the necessary release of an ongoing sensation so pleasurable that it is capable of reducing the mighty sons of Adam to whimpering captives to Wrath.

This fleshly delight of anticipating punishment is sufficient to whip and drive Wrath to a fevered conclusion. The wrathful contemplate the anticipated beaten looks, bowed shoulders, and the wounded spirits of others, just as the gluttonous fantasize a roasted pig or the lustful pour over pornographic pictures. The pleasure is in the anticipation. But as in sex, the actual climax may leave its subject feeling empty and even embarrassed.

The bondage is in the dream. The actual explosion never quite equals the fantasy. It is the exquisite memory of that salacious dream, the delightful anticipation of releasing pent-up Wrath, which brings bondage.

The rapist is the creation of Lucifer. Rape is not sex, but the violent entry of another's body. The instrument of penetration is patently irrelevant; the "pleasure" derived is secondary to the Wrath.

When contemplating the act of rape, the rapist fantasizes not of physical release but of a moment of supreme power. Rape is a living murder, an unequivocal domination, and bold confession: "Now I am the master!" he howls.

Pornography, too, is Lucifer's invention. There is anger in pornography that we angels simply cannot grasp. By the distant rage of pornography, men reduce women to nonhumans. They turn them into cold, slick photos without personalities or lives or thoughts or value. What greater Wrath can be imagined than for a man to dehumanize a woman and subject her soulless body to visual rape by a thousand distant, uncaring eyes!

What greater Wrath can be imagined than for
a man to dehumanize a woman and subject
her soulless body to visual rape by
a thousand distant, uncaring eyes!

Perhaps the strangest aspect of all is the Wrath of whores. Prostitutes, who mutely allow every outrage imaginable upon their persons, often hate beyond measure the men who use them. In fact, the inner rage of prostitutes is such that they secretly delight in the slobbering, subhuman antics of their "customers." They often feel smug and condescending, hating the men who are willing to pay for their bodies. Prostitutes impart their spite, their isolation, and their disease as superior goddesses of death might pour their wrath upon the slaves writhing in hopeless devotion at their stone feet. "Let the suckers pay," becomes the liturgical celebration of Lucifer's destruction in their poor souls.

What a bitter trick Lucifer has played on the "modern" world. By emphasizing the *right* to express anger, he has made humans forget the need to control it. As a result, Wrath savages all other rights except its own undeniable ventilation.

Modern society sides with the angry, identifying with the wrathful. They take vicarious delight in the explosions of others as long as they are distant enough, as in a theater. They snarl, they cheer, and they pay dearly to watch the cinematic Wrath of ex-spouses, crime victims, gunslingers, and nameless psychopaths. Why this willingness to absolve the wrathful? Modern society seems to suffer a corporate schizophrenia.

Society justifies rage at every level and then reels in horror at the Wrath it has unleashed upon itself. Humans seem willing to absolve the rapist because he was angry at his abusive mother; but then they absolve a hate-filled woman because of her anger at rapacious males.

This is the handiwork of Lucifer. He is so full of anger and frustration that he prods the children of Adam as he prodded Cain into fratricide. In his own inadequacy, fear, and impotence, Lucifer drives them with an inner Wrath so deep that it actually dictates much of their lifestyle and values. Their own inner feelings of inadequacy, fueled by fear, produce anger. That anger is the satanic payback of their "modern" mechanical isolation. Their secularization isolates them from their God and their pride separates them from human relationships. Such isolation always creates a traumatic loss of reality. And *that* breeds anger!

We angels watch in horror as Adam's kin dangle on the lonely strands of Lucifer's web. Hanging in space, they are cut off from heaven above and from each other. In that pitiful state he weaves about them the impenetrable cocoon of "justified anger." Boiling inside the darksome little pockets, like so many trapped flies, they repeat their mantra of self-absolution, "I'm mad as hell and I'm not going to take it any more." They finally burst forth as satanic butterflies that have undergone a demonic metamorphosis. Lost souls cut off from heaven and human affection, they careen through their world like time bombs.

Pride is the father of all sin. But in terms of its terrible impact, we of heaven shudder at the effects of Wrath.

What always amazes the angels most is their inexhaustible ability to blame each other. Cain, with his brother's blood on his hands, saw the problem as Abel's "smug, religious superiority." Saul blamed David, then blamed his own son, and finally, God—but never himself.

Pride is the father of all sin. But in terms of its terrible impact, · we of heaven shudder at the effects of Wrath. The record of Lucifer's evil influence upon the history of humanity is painted in blood. Lucifer is a cosmic murderer who, unable to kill God, rages like a petulant brat, pouring his own Wrath into the lives of men. He has always been the same.

He takes special delight in the wrathful for they are his agents of disruption, confusion, intimidation, and fear. I remember Stephen's death. They stood in the street with their fingers in their ears. "Stone him! Stone him!" they screamed.

We angels hovered above. With our wings we feathered sweet grace softly down into Stephen's soul. We had never seen a mortal so full of heaven. Stephen's face! O, Professor, how I wish you could have seen his face. Like what? Adam's? No! No! Adam's was at rest. Stephen's was *glorious!*

You cannot imagine the warfare and the terrible clash. The mob was driven, influenced by Lucifer and a host of demons.

Wrath mixed with Lucifer's laughter poured out in screaming rage.

The stones hit Stephen's body in volley after bloody volley. The murderous rage in the mob was now beyond all reason or sanity. Stephen sank to his knees before the wrathful. The blood ran in his eyes, which gazed heavenward.

Then something wonderful happened in Heaven!

Oh, you cannot understand. Mortals, look above and try to comprehend.

The King Stood Up!

Let the dragon rage and fume. Let his children scream and stop their ears and stone the prophets. Let the devil have his due.

But let this be recorded as well. As Stephen knelt in perfect peace, ministered to by angels, the King of Glory stood up on high.

Dialogue IV:

Lucifer: Violins up. Minor key. Hankies out. Isn't that what you want? Tears of remorse?

Michael: Wrath suffers no remorse!

Lucifer: Exactly! For once you have it. I rejoice at the destruction of the weak. Glee is mine when the gods and goddesses of this present age destroy whatever opposes them.

Michael: Your children are merciless.

Lucifer: Of course! My earth, have you lived in heaven until you've gone soft and senile?! Mercy is only for weaklings.

Michael: Then only weaklings shall obtain mercy.

Lucifer: Not even they! Not from gods and goddesses. When his wife hangs her head and pleads for the "terror" of his Wrath to stop, her husband will not! He is a god.

Michael: He is a monster.

Lucifer: To be sure. Only monsters can be gods. When the pastor's wife begins to crack and tumble toward a breakdown, *my* children will feel nothing—absolutely nothing—but the satisfaction of gods. Let her crack. Let her children weep. There are gods and goddesses in the church who can pound in cold remorseless

Wrath until they get *their* will and until *their* kingdom comes.

Michael: They're sure they're right, of course.

Lucifer: You *are* soft. They're not sure they're right. That isn't the question. They're sure they're gods. The pastor is nothing but the ambassador of the Tyrant, but they are gods. They dare not submit to his authority. He must be crushed by their wrath. He is expected to "be nice," show mercy, tell the truth, endure gossip, and "take up his cross." Well, by all means, let him. My children shall build him one and never look back.

Michael: Your children built the first one.

Lucifer: Yes! What a night! "Crucify him! Crucify him!" What a divine chant. He thinks his children run the church. I laugh in his face.

Michael: Your chain rattling and grimacing is a boring masquerade. This dragon act has never impressed me. I actually preferred your music.

Lucifer: What would you know of that? I took the pipes with me.

Michael: I believe there's a horn lying about somewhere. Let me think. Ah, yes, Gabriel has it.

Lucifer: Oh, that's terrific. Let's go on. Sloth is next on the list.

Michael: Yes, I see it is. Are you sure you want to continue? The more you talk, the less your pretense deceives. You're digging your own pit, to coin a phrase.

Lucifer: My gods deserve to rest. Wrath? That's for some. But Sloth, now *that's* for gods.

CHAPTER EIGHT

Lucifer on Sloth

I am the indolent god; but do not assume that means I am inactive. Activity is hardly the issue. Those who think so cannot begin to comprehend the mind of a god. Sloth is a virtue, so mysterious and so unique in the divine constitution that my own personal history in encouraging it among humanity is very precious to me. Indeed, about no other "sin" will I take greater pains to explain myself.

It is not that Sloth is of greater nobility than Pride or Wrath. But its subtle connection to humanity's search for a divine destiny is frequently overlooked.

For all these centuries I have spread Sloth among Adam's children. I have energetically kneaded Sloth into the lump and timelessly scattered its seeds on the wind. I am constantly active, while being sublimely slothful myself.

Cain was certainly active enough to murder his brother. The point is not necessarily activity or inactivity. The slothful may be quite active, but in their activity they will *care* about nothing. Though they may easily discover what is worth killing for, the slothful will know that nothing, absolutely nothing, is worth dying for. Cain slew Abel because he *cared* nothing for him. Please notice that the Tyrant had no answer for Cain's godliest rhetorical question, "Am I my brother's keeper caretaker, care-giver?" No. The big bully had no answer for that. He simply rejected and exiled mighty Cain, which, of course, did nothing to stop Sloth. The violence of the Tyrant never does stop me nor these great virtues in my children. Cain simply went forth as a god should to found a race who care for nothing.

Pride, Envy, and Wrath turned Cain into a killer god. But Sloth put a smirk on his face.

You may think I make too much of Cain, but then you did not see him as I did. You cannot fully understand his place in human history as the father-god of a race of soulless giants so far above the petty conscience-bound pygmies who suffer in silence. Cain was a god in my own image and I must recognize him. The Tyrant made Adam in his image and Adam proved weak and useless. I birthed Cain from the inside out. He was a cold, uncaring, glacial giant.

See him there pounding the jagged edge of a stone into his brother's stupid skull. As he dies, Abel searches in vain for a hint of mercy in his brother's eyes. It is not there! Cain slew his brother carelessly and then boldly announced his godlike unconcern to the Tyrant. "Am I supposed to *care* for my brother?" What a giant! What a grand, cold, remorseless, unrepentant, uncaring indolent god!

You ask what Cain's fratricide has to do with Sloth? Much, in every way. The Sloth of a true god cares for nothing, values nothing, is impressed with nothing. Hence nothing is worth acting for, working for, waiting for, or enduring for. Sloth is the mother of abortion. Caring nothing for her unborn child, the superior goddess simply announces that she will not endure this. She proves her own divinity by destroying the fruit of her body in favor of Sloth, which is divine self-indulgence.

Through Sloth, I help the gods of the earth to live vicariously. They know they are gods and are willing for hirelings to do their living for them. Politicians, preachers, and entertainers act out the whimsical fantasies of my slothful gods who sit in the balcony of life munching popcorn and gazing down in divine boredom on the whole tired thing. A god must be so far above the concerns, hopes, dreams, fears, and cares of mere humanity that he is bored with it all. A god is bored at funerals, jaded at weddings, unimpressed with heroism, and unmoved by human pathos. These gods and goddesses of Sloth rest unmoved upon life's couch denying any connection at all with the starving in Africa. It is, after all, for the entertainment of the gods that these mortals weep and moan and cling to their wretched little lives. It all has no more meaning to the god of Sloth than a baseball game between two distant cities. He yawns at human agony and switches channels with his remote control. And he is godlike. Cain did not dance around his brother's dead body in some frenzied, primitive celebration of victory. Like the god he was, he simply dropped the rock and strolled listlessly among the trees seeking nothing, hoping nothing, dreaming nothing. He was a god of jaded disinterest.

Pride, Envy, and Wrath turned Cain into a killer god. But Sloth put a smirk on his face. The slothful god gazes condescendingly through half-closed eyes at the droll enthusiasm of mortals. He remains disinterested and utterly unengaged by family gatherings and birthday parties. He mocks at the mere suggestion that he should actually *care* about the needs, fears, hurts, or victories of even his closest relatives. Wrapped in the ermine mantle of divine Sloth, a god would not deign to ask even the most obvious questions of human convention:

"How is mother?" (What a bore!)

"How did your dad's funeral go?" (Oh, please!)

Can you possibly expect a god to be interested in the rustic ceremonies that surround mortal death? And a god would certainly not spend the energy to make even the gesture of an explanation as to why he was not at such a distant and meaningless event as a funeral.

Sloth empowers gods to resist the demands of human society. Mere mortals kowtow to expectations that they work, get educated, learn things, accommodate others, and even feel concern. The god of Sloth looms like a giant above such human vanities. He rules his own universe from a well-padded throne of absolute disinterest.

Kings sit sweatless upon cushions of ease while valets and footmen do their bidding. Mercenaries fight wars for kings and jesters entertain them. Just as the king is the god of the jester, noble sons of Sloth are gods of their television sets. They stare dispassionately as the one-dimensional hirelings on the screen fight, kill, consume, die, and have sex for their entertainment.

Indeed, the tiny screen shrinks the court jesters to a manageable size and the remote control in the god's hand gives him instant power of life and death over the images. What sublime lethargy! What divine power!

King Ahasueras was such a remote control god. Oh, yes, I was instrumental in helping him to find his glory. Ahasueras summoned Vashti (at my suggestion, I humbly add) to appear before him. He reclined in nonchalant resplendence among the lesser gods of his court. (Whenever two or three gods gather in slothful self-indulgence, there am I in the midst of them.)

When Vashti failed to appear instantly on the screen and fulfill her god's desires, she was removed with the flick of Ahasueras' wrist. What a god! One button and the screen switched to Esther.

The laws which dictated appearances in Ahasueras' Persian court were the laws of remote control. If anyone dared (what effrontery!) to appear in King Ahasueras' presence without being summoned, they would be killed instantly unless he extended the scepter in his hand. What Sloth, what monumental, kingly, colossal Sloth! Simply by *not* moving, he was able to do away with his visitors! His *inactivity* ruled in divine deadly power over their most frantic appeals for life.

Ahasueras was not merely a king. He was a god! And I was there. It was I who whispered in his ear to turn blind eyes and deaf ears to the pathetic pleas of those desperate enough to appear unbidden before him. He yawned in godly drowsiness as his soldiers slew the unwanted and unwelcome.

Persia! Now that was a delightful land of Sloth. I know, Michael, you angel-slave, that in your turn you will bring up the unfortunate matter of Esther; but I would simply remind you that one failure does not ruin Ahasueras' otherwise unbroken record of pure Sloth. A record, I might remind you, written in blood.

Indeed, I permanently stationed a Prince of Liberation in Persia's "air" to assist in keeping her gods free from the constant downward gravity of the Tyrant. Oh, you have no conceivable way of understanding how I must fight to keep the gods free of the Tyrant's depraving influence.

In the emperor's box at Rome's great coliseum, I inspired Nero and Caligula in their most sublime moments to casually, uncaringly, divinely twist a wrist and, thumb pointing downward, sentence writhing gladiators to oblivion. Distant from the bloody battles beneath them, they sat like the gods they were and digitally controlled their world with the power of life and death. Reclining on golden couches, unmoved, untouched, and uninvolved, they dictated their entertainments by remote control. *I* was the god of Rome's magnificent Sloth. That Nero fiddled while Rome burned may be more apocryphal than historical. I grant that. I wouldn't want to speak a single untrue sentence. But legend though the story is, it is still a grand compliment to me. In legend, truth is revealed. Bored Imperial Rome dozing through decades of global collapse is proof that the divine disinterest of Sloth had gloriously penetrated Rome's highest offices.

Perhaps the quote of which I am actually the most proud is from King Louis XIV. *"Apres moi, le deluge."* (After me, the flood.) What a god! Utterly and transparently uninvolved with the history of his own nation, Louis announced his divinity. "I am," he boldly said in that one sentence, "above history, above caring, above France. I am GOD! And I do not care."

When I breathed that line into Louis' heart, I hardly dared to hope he might get free enough to actually speak it into existence. But Louis discovered the godlike power in his own tongue. He sliced open the history of France with the proclamation of his own self-actualization. When Louis actually became what he knew he was born for, he set the French aristocracy free to rule as the gods and goddesses of Sloth that they were.

Of course, I know that I cannot count on a Louis in every generation. For example, the geopolitical time is not right for the appearance of an American king-god of Sloth. He may well come, but not yet. The remnants of the Tyrant's wicked spell over America have not been fully broken.

I do not yet occupy an "Emperor's box" at American spectacles nor lead a single king to glorious remote control divinity. But I do sit in a million living rooms and pour sweet Sloth into the lesser gods who loll upon their couches and snuff out a million lives a year with a scepter of Persian power. The remote control device, that allows them to flit from scene to scene and shrink their jesters down to fit in a box in the den, is the modern golden rod of Ahasueras.

Of course, I long for the grand decadence of indolent Rome. But for now, I find the growing Sloth of the Western World sufficient encouragement to go on with the war of liberation. I see what you cannot. I see millions of young emperors enthroned in padded luxury, holding the world and its destiny in push button devices in the palms of their hands. "My kingdom come! My will be done! Bring me another beer!" The gods of the new order will not be kings but school boys and retired mechanics.

The gods of the new order will not be kings but school boys and retired mechanics.

The Sloth of gods transcends the petty rules that bind mortals to plows and math books. A god knows his rights. He will not be hindered by useless and antiquated words of condemnation such as *plagiarism, cheating,* and *larceny.* A god knows that he has a *right* to the "A" without the work, perfection without patience, and success without sacrifice. Mortals may cheat; real gods simply demand their rights.

I see you lift your eyebrows, Professor. You disappoint me. You think I have no morals? How wrong you are. My morals are simply beyond your comprehension. There is no difference between the graduate student who plagiarizes and the armed robber who sticks up a liquor store. They are both gods of Sloth. Both know their rights and they will not be denied. How dare another have an idea, paper, or grade which I do not? How dare they? How dare a mere liquor store have cash while I do not? How dare they indeed?

The pistol in the hand of the slothful god becomes the scepter of Ahasueras, extended or withheld with the power to give and take away life.

I watch in amusement the feeble, futile efforts of humanity to break my gods and strip them of their divine power. Guilt cannot touch a god. There is, therefore, now no condemnation to those who live in Sloth. The truly slothful god can stand and watch unmoved as a neighbor is mugged or murdered. He soars above the common morality of compassion. He soars above all attempts to "motivate" him. Unmoved, untouched, and unfazed, he has put destiny behind him and rises in the arms of sweet deliverance.

I watch in amusement the feeble, futile efforts of humanity to break my gods and strip them of their divine power.

King David was a bitter disappointment to me. When I think of his groveling on the floor in guilt, I feel sick. Even the memory of that disgusting scene is revolting.

"Oh, please forgive me.... Wash me and I shall be whiter than snow.... Purge me with hyssop...." Oh, my dear sweet earth. What pitiful tripe! What a fall. What a tragic end to a king who touched the divine.

He did have his moments, though. One in particular comes to mind, one brief moment of near-divinity that far surpassed all the others. One shining moment of... sloth.

Of course, you thought I would say Lust, didn't you? Indeed, David had his bursts of brilliance in that department. Or perhaps you will remind me of the murder of Uriah the Hittite. But the murder of Uriah was hardly more than a petty child's attempt to hide spilt food by pushing it under the bed. David killed, but then he mourned his actions. He committed adultery, but he wallowed in guilt. This is not exactly the stuff of divinity. He was not a god. He was not even a king. His name should not even be mentioned in the same breath with the warrior god-kings like Caesar, Cyrus, and Alexander the Great.

Yet, for one brief, shining moment, David soared. He rose,

albeit briefly, as high as any god on the wings of Sloth.

"In the season when kings go forth to war, David remained at Jerusalem" (2 Sm 11:1).

A universe of divine Sloth is in that one statement. At least for a moment, David knew that he was born to be god, not a king. Let the others go forth. Let them fight and kill and suffer and sacrifice like the mortals they were. David remained at Jerusalem, resting in the lap of luxury. He strolled the gardens of the palace, indulging for the first time in the delicious sweetmeats of Sloth.

He did nothing!

He strove for nothing!

He worried about, worked at, rose early for, earnestly prayed about, ached for, and wanted for NOTHING!

David stood on the threshold of heaven and saw the glory few men ever know. Nothing stirred him, called him, or restrained him. Bored with war, bored with religion, and bored with wealth and power, David stood on the balcony of his palatial estate and viewed the city with the listless eyes of the truly slothful. And there beneath him the creamy flesh of Bathsheba shimmered in the silvery moonlight.

Lust stirred in his loins, to be sure, but the moment was saturated in divine Sloth. David proved true what I have tried to teach the children of Adam since they escaped from the Garden: *"If nothing holds me, everything is possible."* That one secret makes men into gods. The *nothing* of Sloth quickly translates into the *anything* of lust or greed. Bathsheba was not the chosen trophy of David's Lust. She was the inevitable fruit of his Sloth.

I was there with David on the balcony that night just as I was in the desert with the Hebrew slaves. I whispered on the desert wind and they heard my voice: "Go back to Egypt. Go back to Egypt!"

The slave camps of Goshen do not really gall a god. The slothful god does not mind so much the menial tasks of prison, for there he does not have to think, worry, or decide. The dehumanizing work of a prison is not exactly contrary to Sloth, strange as that may sound. Neither is slavery.

As long as Moses led the way, the dread of the desert was the fact of *being led* in some specific way. The pursuit of some sense of destiny or progress toward a distant land of promise may be a sufficient carrot on a stick to the children of the Tyrant. But such childish inducements are onerous insults to the gods of Sloth. Whose destiny? Whose promise? Who dares to dangle *potential* before a god, to goad him along some painful path to destiny? A god is complete and completely at ease. He cares absolutely nothing for the goals so precious to those slavish mortals who vacuum around his propped-up feet. Better to be a pointless slave in Egypt than to crave the blessings that compel mere mortals to labor and to passion.

"Seek and ye will never be a god.
Ask and ye are less than he who grants.
Knock and the door becomes your bondage."

※※

At this point Michael became more animated than at any previous moment in the entire exchange. He tilted his head as far backward as possible as if to stare directly at the ceiling, and clasped his hands behind his back. After several moments of ponderous silence, Michael sighed a deep, anguished sigh.

"Oh," he moaned, "if only I were not thus commanded!"

"Tsk, tsk, tsk," said Lucifer sarcastically, "do I see just a trace of rebellion?"

"Not rebellion against heaven, Lucifer. Just a longing to be done with you. For the universe to be done with you and your blasphemies," Michael answered. "But the day will come. The *Day will come!*"

"Get on with it, Michael," Lucifer snarled. "On this day you have to answer to my brilliant revelations on this matter of Sloth. You insipid, pathetic lackey of an insipid and colorless Tyrant!"

At that Michael's eyes flashed. He turned directly on me. "I hope you and your computer are ready, Astronomer! That remark is the perfect opening for the truth about Sloth."

CHAPTER NINE

Michael Answers Concerning Sloth

The God of heaven is a being of such grand passion that humanity cannot comprehend it and hell cannot bear it. Humans have an altogether wrong view of God. He is not some placid, pastel cloud of benign but impersonal "force." God is ultimate personhood. He is Being, not idea. He is Presence, not concept. He is Person of magnificent passion, not a cyclical wheel of natural law. God is a King, not a thought; and He has not, and will not, abdicate.

The fallen angels hate the passion of God nearly as much as they hate His holiness. And fallen humanity has so hopelessly confused passion with lust that they are disgusted at the very idea of divine passion when they should tremble in praise.

The love of God is so passionate that the angels weep. The wrath of God kindled against unrighteousness is so terrible that seraphim hide their eyes. The joy of God explodes with such thunderous power that all of heaven quivers with delight.

To angels, the most incomprehensible of all human sins is Sloth. It is monstrously repulsive to see humans in the grip of Sloth. Their morbid inertia mocks at life. They care about nothing. Can they think that being "uncaring" makes them gods? If they could only see as we do the passion of Him who *cares* for them!

The slothful have no life. They are passionless, pitiless, and worst of all, joyless in their existence. I say existence, not life. The slothful are ghosts. They see nothing worth dying for. They will not cry out to God. They will not be excited. They are jaded, bored, disinterested shadows, staring without engagement at the lives of others. Not only are they dead, but they are smug in their death. They mock life.

The slothful have no life. They are passionless, pitiless, and, worst of all, joyless in their existence.

God's caring, compassion, and passion are the very opposite of Sloth. Activity is not the opposite of Sloth; purposefulness is. Inactivity is one part of Sloth, but not the greater part or the worst part. Sloth is the hatred of meaningful work. It is inactivity, not so much of the body as of the intellect, spirit, and will. It is the perversion of peace and serenity.

Father God cares passionately for the least creature in His universe. He could not possibly stand aloof and unmoved from human need. He both cared *and* acted in passion to rescue fallen humanity when its depravity shocked and horrified the hosts of heaven.

We angels live in the very presence of the God of life. He bestirs Himself and the heavens melt like wax. The firmament trembles at His very thoughts and seraphim behold in awe the smoke and thunder of His passion.

For that reason, we angels find it so unimaginable that the children of Adam can watch while another is robbed or murdered. Witchcraft, drugs, and alcoholism drag the slothful into a bondage of dispassionate, untoward pointlessness. The spirit of pornography clutches the slothful in chains of vicarious Lust as they leer at photos of unclad strangers contorted in perverted sex acts. They waste their minds and imaginations on evil. That waste of the imagination alone stuns the angels. Most humans have little or no appreciation for what a grand gift imagination is. When it is wasted on horror and pornography, the angels are speechless.

The slothful even waste their recreation. Far from being re-created, they are gradually spent by their own efforts to be renewed and refreshed. The slothful hate work, but they hurl themselves into pointless play with an awesome ferocity. They are happy to spend and be spent. No distance is too far to travel, no expense too dear, no effort too exacting in pursuit of pursuits without meaning. The slothful weary themselves in pointlessness. They idolize pointlessness. The purposeless activity of the slothful is the god of this present age; meaningful work which creates, constructs, or contributes is its villain.

"The noble Duke of York, he had ten thousand men.
He marched them up the hill and marched them down again."

Symptomatic of the Sloth of the present age is its fascination with shortcuts, gadgets, and ease. The modern age assigns value only to that which makes life *easier.* What makes life *better* is often eschewed as valueless. The remote control device and the garage door opener are valued members of the family, but a physically impaired baby is aborted before she can be born. Had she been allowed to live, she might well have complicated and made life harder for the family. She would almost certainly have brought tremendous pain into their midst. But she might also have enriched them to an extent not possible in any other way.

The slothful gamble away time and prosperity on luck and lotteries, hoping for the wheel of fortune to turn their way. They die in futility cursing "fate" instead of blaming their own Sloth. The slothful live and die as spiritual and emotional midgets. They never grow in grace for they cannot endure growth. Growth involves everything that is hateful to the slothful. Pain, patience, diligence, obedience, and discipline are the keys to growth. Yet, for the slothful these are the enemy. They are to be feared, hated, and abhorred.

The slothful abort their babies, their marriages, their jobs, and even their own lives because they will not suffer the pain, pay the price, exert the effort, or endure the wait that would have allowed them to grow. Obsessed with retirement, relaxation, and rest, they live weary, puny lives, constantly waiting for the unfulfilled pipe dream, the ship that never comes in, and the gamble that never pays off. They descend by the steps of "get rich quick schemes" into the basement of poverty.

By avoiding the pain and the price of life, they gradually lose track of its reality. They live a colorless, tasteless, tearless life of sweet repose. And having found it, they find themselves to be the plastic replicas of living souls. Reality avoided loses its ability to inform life with truth. The most unreal of all are the miniature men and women whose work is Sloth and whose rest is death. They are mutant test-tube fruit of a plastic age.

What shocks angels about Sloth is not that it makes life evil, like Wrath or Greed or Lust. More horrible, Sloth trivializes life. The slothful equate movies with issues and theme parks with prayer meetings. They cannot make commitments to actually *do* anything. Parenting shrivels because it takes discipline to lovingly train another. It is easier to indulge a child than to shape his character. "Giving in" is the path of least resistance, least effort, and least love. Chastening, teaching, rebuking, and even properly punishing a child takes time, perseverance, and sacrifice. To give him what he pleads and weeps and screams for costs very little.

Relationships likewise shrink because they exist in a sterile box of effortlessness. As soon as difficulties arise, a relationship must either end or the parties involved tacitly agree to walk only on a few safe pathways. But friends who can walk together only through clover and never through thorns, never share blood and agony. It is in these difficulties that friendships grow deep and strong. Marriages that self-destruct at the first blush of pain or hardship are a tragic testimony to an age that glorifies Sloth and despises endurance.

⚔

> *Marriages that self-destruct at the first blush of pain or hardship are a tragic testimony to an age that glorifies Sloth and despises endurance.*

⚔

Sloth creates a culture reaching for the mirage of success without work. Such a culture hates the classical, for it cannot create true beauty with the seeming effortlessness of genius. Therefore, it staples an empty can of tomato soup to a canvas and calls it art. It reduces its own language to the bland oatmeal of street jive, advertising jingles, and scientific nomenclature. Sloth recreates culture in the image of society's least creative, least beautiful, least productive, and least disciplined. The art of Sloth is bastardized by the idolatry of Sloth which is ease. The slothful "artist" finds he has a "talent" for depicting a crucifix plunged in urine. Slothful art critics refuse to denounce it as the perversion it is. And a slothful society calls it art because it will not even expend the mental and moral energy necessary to discern and discriminate.

Slothfulness is the sin of neglect. Lucifer delighted in telling how he "inspired" Cain to murder his righteous brother. Let him also record the cold, hollow death in Cain's listless stare as he beheld the blood of his brother soaking into the sand. Let him record the monstrousness of eyes that look on death without compassion and do murder with a yawn.

Lucifer calls Sloth a virtue and its slaves gods. Let him tell of the slothful whose need drives them into sexual excess, not from Lust but from emptiness. Let him tell of the staring ghosts who pour narcotic death into their own bloodstream, not from Lust for sensation but from spiritual death that cries for a magic elixir to give life. Let Lucifer tell of young women who kill their "inconvenient" babies in the morning and go to the movies in the afternoon.

Sloth is the most joyless of all sins. Pride is Lucifer's attempt to kill God. Sloth is his effort to kill joy. Pride delights in the death of Jesus. Sloth is bored with the resurrection.

The God of Passion will not endure the passionlessness of Sloth. What some men call mature, heaven calls lukewarm. The wrathful will be hurled into outer darkness by the hand of God. The slothful will be spewed out of His mouth.

Dialogue V:

Lucifer: You turn everything topside down.

Michael: Indeed?

Lucifer: Yes. Do I bewitch them with sorcery, or does the Tyrant? Is religion not the most addictive opiate of all?

Michael: *You* decry religion? Shall wolves denounce howling? Religion is your specialty. *You* would make the Bride a whore. You would steal the worship of heaven from her heart and make her strut upon a stage. You paint her eyes, and give her robes, and make her lust for show and glamour and sensual experience. From the cool, dark velvet death, a candle-lit and berobed religiosity of excess and carnal embarrassment puts the cup of flesh to her lips and steals the cup of blood.

Lucifer: The church is...

Michael: Will you teach on the church? I think not. The King has allowed you to sport this nonsensical tripe about these sins in order to let you talk until you have nowhere to hide. But do not overstep your bounds! Religion is the subject.

Lucifer: We were talking about Sloth, in case you forgot.

Michael: What's the difference? Sloth steals their souls' desire. Unable to shake themselves and rise to seek His face, they help themselves to willing doctors who will inject them with the serum of Sloth. Religion, like a lullaby, makes men too lazy to live. Or else they find an organ grinder with a dancing monkey on a string, and look at the monkey! Look at the monkey dance! See how funny!

And Heaven weeps.

They cry, "Make us laugh! Bring out the gypsy dancing girls. Now something new. Something new! We would laugh and dance and play," they shout! "Energy enough to watch but not to pray. Now, Monkey, make us laugh and laugh and laugh." Slothful souls unable to seek a Holy King find solace in glitsy entertainment.

And Heaven weeps.

You, Lucifer, you are no god at all, but just a lazy deceiver who thinks the play's the thing. And you make your children laugh until they weep from emptiness, and dance until they die. Do NOT speak to me of religion! You are the father of that carnival show.

Lucifer: Well, I must say. I am shocked. This display…

Michael: Please, spare me. This is a farce. Now, let me regain my composure while you tell lies about gold.

Lucifer: Lies? Never! Gold? Now, that's a glistering word.

CHAPTER TEN

Lucifer on Greed

I am the god of gold. I am the god of more—and more, and more. Sufficiency is the monstrous deception of the Tyrant perpetrated upon unsuspecting humanity. It is his ungodly effort to anesthetize them to their own desires. He wants men to be pacified, placated, satiated, dull-witted. He wants placid hypocrites who are unable to say even to themselves, "I want."

I want gods who are in touch with their desires, who know what they desire! I want gods and goddesses who are unafraid of glitter and glamour. I wish to set women free to see that what they want is of infinite importance. A true goddess knows that she *is* her own desires. A god knows that gold is real, gold is earnest, and that gain is the goal!

Greed is not the dirty word the Tyrant pretends it to be. Indeed, he knows Greed is a key to liberation for the children of Adam. Only the truly avaricious can see through the wicked ruse of heaven's current occupants. The Tyrant requires the "faithful" to mouth such banality as, "Give us this day our daily bread."

Greed puts the pin to that pompous balloon right enough! What a preposterous precept! Shall gods and goddesses *ask* for anything? Furthermore, the whole idea of "daily" bread reeks of having just enough to get by. The greedy see through that and know it is a trap. Once a human sinks to that level of bare necessity met on a daily basis, he is doomed! My earth, it shocks me to know that any of the children of Adam have ever prayed such nonsense.

But I am a realist. They do pray. They will, I know, as long as the Tyrant's superstition grips whole cultures in guilt and fearful dependence.

The Tyrant says, "Blessed are the poor in spirit."

I say, "Cursed are the poor in *anything*." The greatest curse of all is to *need* that which can be supplied only by the very hand which denies me my divinity.

Greed is the ladder up from spiritual slavery. The mantra of the greedy is, "Everything's for Sale." My power, my office, my influence, my name, my body, my soul—ALL FOR SALE!"

The avaricious know that they can sell only that over which they have dominion. A man is lord of his castle only if he can sell it. A woman is mistress of her person only when she can sell it. A senator is in bondage to his office if it owns him. If he owns it, then he is the god of the senate and he profits thereby.

❧❧

The mantra of the greedy is, "Everything's for Sale."
My power, my office, my influence, my name,
my body, my soul—All For Sale!

❧❧

The Tyrant paints prostitutes as pathetic victims of oppression. What a lie! A prostitute is a goddess. She is in control. She is a vengeful goddess of gold. She dominates the man who uses her. He must have her. She is the object of his Lust. His gold is the object of her Lust. Control and gain in one act of prostitution. Divine! He goes away an empty, sheepish, deprived customer. She leaves a mocking, enriched goddess counting his gold and despising his need of her.

Not all whores are goddesses but, in one way or another, all goddesses are whores. I delight in the whore-gods (male or female) for whom no gain is enough.

Greed makes gods of capitalists. The great American "robber barons" were warrior kings. They were gods of avarice. They knew what only the anointed few ever discover. They defined themselves by their own desire for wealth.

John D. Rockefeller's ruthlessness in building the Standard Oil monopoly was not just good business. He was a god of Greed. In 1869, Jay Gould single-handedly caused a nationwide financial panic in the United States by his efforts to corner the gold market. His transportation and communication empire gained and gained and gained. He was a god of gain and he knew it! J. P. Morgan's U.S. Steel and International Harvester trusts were god-wrought cities built foursquare. They had no need of a sun, for Morgan was the lamp thereof. Oh, what gods!

For a god of Greed, wealth is not a means to an end. It is an end in itself. The wealth of gods is the knowledge that they *are* what they own. It is not merely a matter of buying things. That is the Greed of paper boys.

The great gods of gold are living monuments to self-creation which is the essence of all freedom from the Tyrant. The "self-made" owes no gratitude to Providence and no debt to society. He has scratched enough gold out of the bowels of the earth, or out of the teeth of humanity, to fashion an idol in his own image. He erects it on the Plain of Shinar like the statue of Nebuchadnezzar and commands the mortals to worship. He has made himself. He is the creation of his own Greed. Defined by his possessions, he is the sheep of his own pasture. He bows to no god but himself, for only a god can create himself.

The gods of Greed are not all rich. That is hardly the point. A man who is defined by the gold he *wants* is no less a god of Greed than the one who is defined by the gold he *has*.

I have slaved throughout the ages to free the race of Adam

from its perverted obsession with the spiritual, I have worked without hope of personal gain or glory to hand to the gods of the earth a material kingdom. But my enemy, the Tyrant, has sown tares in the field. It is his trick to deprive them, of course, thereby insuring their dependence upon him. You see how he wants Eve's children to beg and plead for their bread. Disgusting!

It was so from the very beginning. He forbade Adam and Eve what they really wanted, hence defining them by his will. But *I* set them free. *I* taught them to *want*. Defined by His will, Eve was a slave. Defined by her desire, she became the goddess she was destined to be.

The Tyrant wants humans to be fixated on the spiritual. He wants them to be useless, dispossessed, penniless refugees in the earth. With their eyes on heaven and their heads in the clouds, praying prayers he will not answer, they become dependents. He wants esoteric camp followers of heaven without two pennies to rub together, wrapping themselves in wretched skins that he provides.

You see, the moment Adam and Eve took the single fruit by their own initiative, he was furious. That is the Tyrant. From the Garden onward, I have worked tirelessly to teach humanity self-dependence. I must assist them to find a wholesome material view of a material universe. Humans must be helped upward to self-made status where they redefine and constantly reinvent themselves in terms of what they earn or own or spend.

I must constantly help them to see the material possibilities. If I fail to open their eyes to the more that may be theirs, they will sink into hopeless spirituality. I must remind them of the bigger and better, the more expensive and the more exclusive, or they will lose sight of the vision. Of course, mere possessions are not the whole answer, but they are useful in motivation.

Unless I increase their materialism, the Tyrant will constantly shrink their worldview. He speaks to them of need. I of want. He summons them to moderation (more rules). I call them to a higher plane of material self-invention called consumption. He speaks of giving, I of having.

The gods of this age know that gratitude inhibits Greed. Contentment emasculates it, and mercy softens it.

Whether a god flaunts his wealth or hoards it is absolutely irrelevant. By flaunting wealth, he announces his divine right as a god. By hoarding it, he denies anyone else's claim against him. Who, after all, dares to put a finger on the sacred possessions of a self-made god? Who, indeed?

Gradually these gods and goddesses can rise on golden wings into that rarified atmosphere of the exalted morality of the divine. The true gods, the great, rare gods of Greed know that the common laws of right and wrong (what can that mean anyway?) apply only to day laborers and salaried employees.

The gods of wealth sit in luxurious offices and conspire to sell tainted baby food to the Third World. They are not murderers. They are gods! More than one congressman has taken laundered money from Central America to build more stately mansions. But the true whore-god among them all is the one who does it in the knowledge that he is totally justified. The house, after all, is the house of a god.

The preacher who runs off with the offering may be greedy. He shows promise, to be sure, and I can work with him. But only a god of majesty can preach with pure conviction a gospel of gain. Not for ten million bloodless bankers would I trade such a trophy of the material truth. Such a god in the pulpit makes a doctrine of my truth and proclaims it in the name of the Tyrant.

You cannot imagine how I must fight against the pathetic, primordial urges of humanity. Something dark and sinister in the race of Adam continues to be subject to such beggarly impulses as gratitude, mercy, and contentment. One would think that after countless centuries of ceaseless effort, I might have rooted out such loathsome instincts.

Nevertheless, the gods of this age are above such darkness. They know that gratitude inhibits Greed. Contentment emasculates it, and mercy softens it. Mercy will invariably cost something. Gods run up bills and put them on the credit card. Gods borrow and leverage and leave. The merciful pay. They always pay. Shall a god pay? Nonsense. He receives tribute; he does not grant it. Let the merciful pay the bills.

I open the eyes of my own. They are my children and they know my voice. They long for more. They are gods in my image who have ripped their lives free from bondage and weak vassalage to others, to ethics, to spirituality, and to the Tyrant. They reign supreme with their eyes fixed on the roulette wheel, the Lotto numbers, or the Dow Jones Report. As free as only gods can be, they clutch their just deserts and scream into the oppressive face of the Tyrant, "These things are mine!"

I was at the elbow of Judas Iscariot at the very moment he ripped himself free. For three years, Judas struggled against the inflated spirituality and otherworldliness of the Princeling Jesus. Earth, what an absolute burlesque show!

"The Son of Man has nowhere to lay his head."

"Consider the lilies of the field."

"Lay not up for yourselves treasures on earth."

(I am only quoting. Please do not take offense.)

What crass hypocrisy! When Jesus wanted more, he brought forth gold out of the fishes' mouth. When *he* wanted more, he used his exalted spirituality at will. But when anyone else wanted more, he flew into a rage.

Finally, he went too far, of course. I stood at Judas' elbow as Jesus whipped the money-changers out of the temple. I explained the situation as it really was and Judas had ears to hear.

"Observe," I said, "how he drives them out with a fury. What have they done? Do they deserve such treatment because they want a living? Is he the only one who deserves to get anything out of this?"

I must be modest. I must restrain myself. But the truth is inescapable even if it appears a bit self-congratulatory. My words seemed to fill Judas' heart with a knowledge of the truth which set him free.

Standing there watching the shocking scene before him, Judas Iscariot knew two things. He knew Jesus was going to deprive them all. The whole, wild three years was going to end in some spiritual madness, and he and the other followers of Jesus were going to walk away empty-handed. Well, he had not invested three years of his life to see it all destroyed by a leader who refused to consider the material needs of his devoted followers.

Second, Judas saw that he was a god. He stood completely alone in the temple that day. No one could possibly touch him. He was a god. He had *rights*! He *deserved*...

Thirty pieces of silver was all it took to buy his own divinity. It was not the money—it was the price of freedom. He would never again wander barefoot like a beggar. He was free! He was as god.

Stand fast, therefore, in the liberty wherewith I have made you to stand. Do not go back into bondage. You are the god of what you can sell. Open, therefore, my child, and count the pieces, one through thirty. If you are for sale, I will fill your hand with the price of a god.

CHAPTER ELEVEN

Michael Answers Concerning Greed

L ucifer wanted to hold the wealth of this world. Well—he holds it. But not for long. He wants to drag the sons of men down into the spiritless darkness of his own material world. Lucifer longs to tear the eyes of Adam's children away from God and fix them in avaricious Lust upon material wealth. Nothing will satisfy him but the flame of Greed that burns the life of God out of the children of the King.

"O Lucifer, you evil star, how the mighty are fallen! What was it you desired? You were the son of the morning, beautiful and glorious! The music in your pipes was without equal as you walked up and down in the midst of heaven's glory."

The tragedy of Satan is not simply that he became an evil angel. It is that he traded heaven for the material world. He gave up that which was eternal for that which was temporary at best. The arrogance of Lucifer is self-worship.

Shall he be able to record his end? He knows it well enough and he trembles at the very thought. The sentence has been passed and the decree has been handed down from on high. Let him write of his destiny. Let the mighty Lucifer record his fear of the flames that will be his eternal home!

Avarice is satanic in both its nature and its end. The greedy look more like Lucifer than they can imagine. In one form, of course, Greed hoards. Stinginess is social Greed that withholds. Greed denies life, joy, others, and even oddly enough, *self* for the sake of possessing wealth. It is no wonder that the words *miser* and *misery* share a common root. A miser is a wretched person indeed. Wretched is the misery and loneliness of one who clutches gold's cold metal for comfort and delights more in the clink of coins than in the laughter of children.

The tragedy of Satan is not simply that he became an evil angel. It is that he traded heaven for the material world.

Greed may flaunt wealth as well as hoard it. The exorbitant tip is greed's backhand. The movie star may slap a hundred dollar tip into the hand of an hotel clerk not from spontaneous generosity as much as to make a statement. "*I have,*" he announces. "I have so much that this which means a great deal to you, means nothing to me."

As much with his cavalier attitude as with the size of the tip, the wealthy star announces himself, "I am what I have. I relate only by what I have and hence who I am." By flaunting his wealth, he displays his Greed for all to see.

Greed is more than having *things*. It is *having* things. The difference is subtle. Greed takes joy not in the things, but in knowing that I *have* the things and that others *know* I have them. There is a Greed which is flamboyant and showy. To possess is not enough. Wealth must be worn, driven, eaten, or sailed for all to see.

There is also a kind of Greed that is a secret, sensual lust to simply possess. Such private Greed is inflamed by the very idea that there is a toy anywhere it does not have. The affluent young couple who sit with a luxury catalog open on their laps are not dreaming so much of having what they need or even what they want. They are merely dreaming of having and having and having. They study to know what others have. They are well-versed in what brands, styles, and colors are "right" to have. They even have the "right" catalog.

The greedy may not care how good the clothing is as much as how good the label is. Finally the label in his shirts becomes the label in his life. He must read it over and over again to reassure himself. "I have. I am because I own. I have. I am what I have."

The gifts of the greedy are frank denials of love. They do not give for the pleasure of those who receive. The greedy give the gifts which give *them* pleasure. With the gift they do not make a statement of love or friendship or even generosity. Rather, they restate who they are and reassure themselves by the very price that they are what they have.

The desire of the greedy for material wealth so thoroughly defines life that they lose all sense of themselves apart from what they have. Hence Greed reinforces itself over and over again. Having, spending, hoarding, getting, having, spending... becomes a nightmare cycle of self-definition.

Driven by avarice, the greedy deny all reason and reality. Their need to have a new car argues that the payments would be less than the monthly repair bills on the one they have. No amount of proof will persuade them, because Greed is not about arithmetic. It is about having more.

To the avaricious, needlessness actually feels like great need. Greed creates a gradual loss of reality and self-deception. When greedy people say they need a fur or a luxury automobile or a vacation home in Florida, they are not lying. They are deceived. The deceitfulness of riches is very supernatural and extremely powerful.

Strange, indeed, to angels is the connection between Sloth and Greed. Inherited wealth does not necessarily create Sloth, but it does create an atmosphere that is highly conducive to it. The Sloth which springs full-grown in many who inherit fortunes may be in constant, lifelong, unresolved conflict with their Greed. The resulting dysfunction is a neurotic love-hate relationship the slothful have with the wealth they inherit. They hate who they are because who they are is what they have. What they have drives them to *do,* and Sloth hates *doing.* What a pathetic cycle!

It is a strange and horrible thing for angels to watch the pitiful creatures dangling on the tenterhook of Sloth turning in the gale force winds of Greed! They want more and receive less at the same time. They want more wealth and have less life. These are the pitiable greedy who etch themselves one-dimensionally on flat, cold, precious-metal planes.

The depersonalization of Greed is particularly sad. The greedy simply lose track of themselves as they gradually become what they own. They fade into pale ghosts who actually *are* what they wear and drive. They now must act as someone should who owns such a coat or drives a certain car.

The greedy simply lose track of themselves as they gradually become what they own.

Why do so many of them hate their jobs? Because they are driven by Greed, and work is the price that must be paid. If they give in to Sloth, they may not *have,* so they keep working, sometimes with a fury. They hate work as a slave always hates his master, but their Greed compels them onward.

Why is there so much adultery among the rich? The usual reasons, of course, go without saying. Lust, ease of opportunity, and

Sloth contribute; but the crucial reason is the search for meaning. The depersonalization of Greed creates shadowy people who hate themselves, their jobs, and their relationships. In sexual liaisons, they hope to find some significance. The affair itself is not really that important, except as it offers hope for meaning.

In the same sense, the greedy are often uncharacteristically devoted to one "cause" after another. This may not seem to fit at first glance, but it is symptomatic of their search for meaning. Perhaps they sense instinctively that they can find in a *cause-célèbre* the self they prostituted and lost track of in their Greed. They now give time and money compulsively hoping to discover some goodness in themselves. By hurling themselves into saving whales or stopping the fur trade, they hope to find what they long ago sold.

In truth, there is little mercy among the rich. And do you know why? If I am defined by what I own, then the loss of one single cent is a threat to who I am. If my very existence is diminished by the tiniest loss, I cannot afford to pity the poor.

The worst thing about Greed is its power to force humanity downward. Greed drives out all vision but its own. It allows no nobility of purpose, no grand dream apart from wealth, and affords no latitude for generosity or graciousness of spirit.

The prostitute mocks the God who created her. By selling herself, she declares her temple to be of less intrinsic value than her customer's paper money. In other words, it does not matter what anyone does to her body as long as that person pays for the privilege.

The greedy businessman is no less a prostitute. With the cold eyes and smug leer of a street corner whore, he conspires with his lawyer to launch an "intimidation law suit," knowing that the defendant cannot afford a long drawn-out suit. They split their take like hoods in an alley and lose themselves in the process. The sins of business make soulless ghosts of men. They gradually fade year after year until at the end, no one can see them and they themselves see nothing when they look in the mirror.

The angels know what men refuse to admit—that Greed and murder always hold hands. The civil servant who sells to the black market the food meant for the poor is not just greedy. He is a murderer. He is perfectly willing that the poor children for whom the food is intended famish without it.

The hoarder, the waster, the whore, and the greedy are all the same. The hoarder denies the good use of his gold. The waster, by poor use, does the same. The hoarder destroys others by denying them. The waster pours the answer to the needs of others down rat holes of sin and foolishness. Greed kills. It kills gratitude, contentment, and joy.

There is the thug who wastes the life of a gas station owner for thirty dollars so he can waste the money on marijuana. Life, family, futures, happiness, hopes, and dreams lie at his feet oozing onto the floor of a gas station office. He stands above the body, not as a powerful giant but as a greedy, murderous ghost. He is no different than the corporate executive who dumps tainted baby food in the Third World or the male prostitute who laughs as he opens himself to another man knowing that the slow death of AIDS lurks in his own flesh.

The greedy see a "For Sale" sign on all of life. They themselves have been for sale for so long that they cannot imagine anyone or anything that is not for sale. The prostitute comforts herself that she and the housewife are the same—she just gets paid in cash and the housewife in room and board.

Her eyes are so dirtied by Greed that she cannot comprehend the beauty and holiness of the marriage covenant. She has no idea of how the King feels about a marriage bed that is pure and undefiled. The prostitute knows nothing of loving, passionate, beautiful, tender sex, for she sold her birthright. Her only comfort is to brand housewives as polite whores.

Greed has now gutted so many ministries that we angels simply cannot understand why the church below does not *see* it. Perhaps it *will not see*. Greed in ministry is not all about getting rich off the gospel. It is far more often about the material replacing the hand of the King.

Simon the Magician offered Peter and John money for a powerful, public ministry. "Give me also this power, that on whomsoever I lay hands, he may receive the Holy Ghost."*

Peter sensed the horror of heaven and felt the wrath of the King. His discernment was clear, powerful, and all together righteous.

"Thy money perish with thee," Peter said, "because thou hast thought that the gift of God may be purchased with money."

A man's Greed in ministry is revealed by what he hopes to *buy* even more than by what he hopes to gain. Greed is about the *use* of money as much as about hoarding it. The minister whose ethics are eaten away by Greed reveals his corruption by materialistic shortcuts. He borrows to live at too high a standard, then welshes on the debt. He believes that he can buy the building or the air time or the publicity that will "give him the power."

❈

Greed is about the use *of money as much as about hoarding it.*

❈

He is stunned when heaven itself or even another man or ministry says, "No! Not for sale!" He feels condemned and even shocked at the response. He literally cannot understand. He has bought and sold everything for so long that his perceptions and worldview are entirely materialistic. His emphasis in public ministry may well be upon signs and wonders, miracles and methods, while his heart and hopes rest upon the material. He is rapidly

*Acts 8:19 KJV

becoming a ghost and does not even see himself disappearing.

This same face of Greed collides in the soul of laypersons at such a tangential angle that many fail to discern it as such. That angle, the use of generosity for personal gain, is basically the same sin as using money to "buy" into ministry.

Ananias and Sapphira were hypocrites. They were envious, power-hungry, position-seeking hypocrites. But their Greed was evident in their materialism. They conspired to keep enough to "make them happy," gave enough to "make them famous," and lied enough to "look spiritual."

Like the minister who hopes to purchase fame, they hoped to purchase reputation in the community of faith without using faith. They hoped to purchase favor with the King by using the currency of earth. Some of the largest gifts ever offered are despised by heaven, for they cloak hidden agendas, controlling spirits, and Greed. Some of the smallest are accepted, for they reveal generosity and joy in simply being allowed to give.

The evangelist who raises millions by deception is greedy. Angels gape at his Lust for money. But just as ugly are the thousands who send in "offerings" to buy a financial miracle. They play the religious lotto, betting on "miracle ministries" and waiting for heaven to draw the numbers. They do not give to glorify the King, to win the lost, or to comfort the poor and hurting. They give to get. They play the game of religious Power Ball and desire to "give a testimony" before the eyes of men. As dead as Ananias and Sapphira, they write their checks, but there is no life in them.

Wretched Judas stared at the thirty pieces of silver in the palm of his hand. As insanity tightened its grip he asked himself, "Could *I* have sold the Son of Man for thirty pieces of silver?"

He needn't have wondered. In Times Square the angels stand and weep and then turn their faces to the wall as sons and daughters are sold for much less a thousand times a day.

Dialogue VI:

Lucifer: You make gold sound like dirt.

Michael: The One who makes gold made dirt. They are the same to me.

Lucifer: Ah, but not to them. Not to our typist. (Here Lucifer indicated me with a disdainful head bob.)

Michael: If the earth were made of gold, men would kill for a spoonful of dirt.

Lucifer: I love it.

Michael: Gluttony must come next.

Lucifer: Of course. Greed with a greasy smile.

Michael: I know this will be disgusting.

Lucifer: I hope so, brother. I certainly hope so.

CHAPTER TWELVE

Lucifer on Gluttony

I am the god of the belly. Please do not underestimate such a simple statement. I did not say the god of the stomach. That is true, but too restrictive. I am the god of the belly.

The belly is that bank of all human appetites. The belly is the soul of the carnal god. The paradox of those who become belly gods is so mysterious and so wonderful that my own saliva flows in the very explanation. As a man becomes a god, his eyes are gradually opened to see that every appetite is sacred. His belly is a god unto itself because it is *his* belly. *That* is the kingdom of the gods.

If a god's belly is also a god, then devouring is holy in every way. The cannibals have been much maligned. The Christian moralists have made humanity think of cannibalism as some horrible, base perversion by primitive tribes. They try to paint disgusting pictures of savagery. But let me set the record straight. What sweeter food for a god than the flesh of a god? Since the beginning of things, the more nearly men became gods and the closer those gods came to me, the closer they came to cannibalism.

Idi Amin was not merely the dictator of Uganda. He was the god of Uganda. Amin was excoriated in the world press as a "monster" because of his cannibalism. He was not condemned for "mass murder," whatever that means. He was condemned for heresy. He announced his divinity and fed the god-self of his own belly with the food of gods. I was there to light his soul. Earth, what a giant! He ate his own people! His belly was his god. *He* was their god. Let them worship.

The light of a thousand primitive bonfires danced in his eyes as Idi Amin became an incarnate god. He found out what my children have known for thousands of years—the belly of a god must not be denied. The belly of a god *is* a god and must not be denied anything. Indeed, it must be worshiped.

The Lust to consume is the passion of gods. It has always been my premise that any person may become a god. That does not mean they all start as gods. They may not soar to such heights as Amin did, but still they are on their way to becoming gods. After that, of course, it is merely a matter of degree.

I take great satisfaction in pointing out that I have graced a million banqueting tables. In fact, any unbiased historian worth his salt would be forced to admit that the entire history of humanity is actually the story of food. And I am at the very center of that story. From the time of Adam, I have striven to enlighten the gods of the earth. They must come to understand that a god denied is but a slave.

I reasoned with Eve ever so gently. I am, after all, a gentleman. It is the Tyrant of heaven with whom negotiation is impossible. He said, "Thou shalt not eat of such and such a fruit."

I refuse to be drawn into useless arguments about which fruit. I leave such quibbling to the Tyrant and his pulpit pirates. Fruit of this, fruit of that—what conceivable difference does it make?

"Thou shalt not eat of the fruit..." is what the Tyrant said. No discussion. No room for debate. Utterly unreasonable! That is the Tyrant's way.

What a hypocrite the Tyrant is! "Come let us reason together," he says in his book of lies. What brazen hypocrisy! He will not be reasoned with. His word is law.

But I am a reasonable god. I helped Eve understand the Tyrant's lies. I reasoned with her, god to goddess. I brought freedom into the Garden of Tyranny and shed light on the face of deceit. Eve recognized the truth when she heard it. She knew she would not die, and that she and the man were destined for divinity. All she needed was the voice of reason and she would not deny her belly.

It is strange to me how the Tyrant weaves threads of truth among the lies of his Bible.

"And when the woman saw she would not die and that the fruit was good to eat and desirable to make one wise, she did eat."*

Please notice that the Tyrant hoped to deny Eve's belly as well as her divinity. What a monster! I wanted her to eat her way to freedom—and she did.

I have helped a million gluttonous gods since then. The Romans were master gluttons. Ah, I do miss those orgies. How wistful I become even thinking of them now. They would eat until their bellies simply could not hold anymore, then induce vomiting and start all over. What gods!

They knew that the craving of the belly of a god is sacred in and of itself. Food is not holy except as it goes into the belly of gods. Therefore, food is not the issue and must not be allowed to interfere with the belly's cravings. That would be a horrible idolatry.

The Romans made a holy feast of the banquet table by moving beyond such insipid thoughts as nourishment, fullness, and satisfaction. They knew the table was not meant for food but for worship, and their bellies were gods. Worship and worship and worship and then vomit and worship again. That was what made the Romans into gods. Bacchus was their name for the god of drunkenness, feasting, and frolic. Ah, I do so miss the Romans.

---

*(Genesis 3:6). Note: This is not the authorized version, but Lucifer insisted it be printed this way. The reader is invited to compare.

The truly gluttonous god is not nearly so concerned with food as you might think. Eve did not eat the forbidden fruit because she was hungry. Hunger is the appetite of a mortal. Eve ate the forbidden fruit because her belly craved the food of gods. Her flesh-self longed for free expression as a goddess.

In the beginning was the flesh and the flesh craved. And that craving devoured and became a goddess and dwelt among us. And we beheld her gluttony as of the gluttony of the first of many divine daughters who know that their bellies are gods.

Perhaps the most maligned of all the theological refugees of history are those modern daughters of Eve known as bulimics. My heart goes out to them. They are pitiable casualties of the Tyrant's war on gluttony. They eat and then sneak like thieves into their bathrooms to vomit. They hide their gluttony as if it were some wicked secret.

The terrible thing is to watch them die. The Tyrant comes to steal and to kill and to destroy. I strive to help them but, of course, the shame and secrecy denies them what they need which is, quite simply, *more.*

Christianity kills those with food addictions. By labeling them as abnormal and neurotic, Christianized society sentences them to secret death. I would give them public orgies. Christianity calls it bondage and excess. Ludicrous! What is excess for a goddess?

Christianity also thus killed the Roman Empire. It is no coincidence that as Christians ended the Roman food orgies, the empire collapsed. When Christians replaced the gusty, lusty gluttony of Rome with their prissy meal of bread and wine, the divine empire of holy gods cracked open and crumbled. Rome was not conquered by the Huns and Visigoths. It was conquered by communion.

There is no food for the belly in Christian communion. How can the Tyrant call the cannibal a primitive beast, then invite his followers to feed on him and drink his blood? He speaks out of both sides of his mouth, as usual.

The point of Christian communion is not partaking but deny-ing. Even in amount the whole thing is a farce. The smidgen of bread and tiny sip of wine are expressive of this.

The belly of a god will not be filled by a symbolic feast for sissies. If flesh, then let it be real flesh. If blood, then real blood. If bread, then more and more.

I do see signs of hope among the moderns. There are those whose gluttony simply will not be denied. They generally fall into two groups.

First are the gluttons in terms of sheer amount. What kings and gods are those who refuse to bow to the limits of polite soci-ety or popular Christianity! Refusing to be intimidated by the "needs of the hungry," they rightfully claim their status as gods. At a million smorgasbords, they eat prodigious amounts without thought or concern for taste or quality. The ravenous gluttons of the modern era are not French aristocrats, but truck drivers who eat six hot dogs, a bowl of chili, two bottles of beer and three Moon Pies. They eat like gods with their bellies bulging obscene-ly before the hungry eyes of the starving masses.

"Let them eat cake!" they snarl. They are the godlike godsons of Marie Antoinette, the patroness of gluttons.

These are not prissy gourmets with their pinkie fingers curving delicately away from tiny china cups of perfectly brewed tea. These are gods with bellies. They know gluttony for what it is— the belly-virtue of the gods of flesh.

I do have a second great hope for modern gluttons, however. To reclaim its rightful niche as modern virtue, Gluttony must, in some other circles, be removed from the good wholesome, belly-bulging gorgers of fast food. *I* approve of them heartily, for it is in their image that Bacchus was fashioned. But among prissier gluttons, that sort is seen as embarrassing and uncouth.

But that, in fact, presents no serious problem to the promulga-tion of the virtue of Gluttony. Indeed, it offers me a unique opportunity to translate this great virtue into more sophisticated terms that can be appreciated by the daintier elements of society. Gluttony then, in its primal form, is simply the demand for *more*. But it is also the virtue that demands *perfection*. This subtler form is the stuff of goddesses. Bulk is the demand of Bacchus and his modern ballgame gods, but perfection is the Gluttony of gourmets. More! Better! More perfection! More, more, more!

The ravenous gluttons of the modern era are not French aristocrats, but truck drivers who eat six hot dogs, a bowl of chili, two bottles of beer, and three Moon Pies.

See her there at her table in a fashionable restaurant on Rodeo Drive. She is a goddess of perfection. Her perfect clothes and perfect hair match her perfect figure. Svelte and trendy, she is profoundly aware that she is a goddess. She glances at her reflection in the mirror on the wall. Perfect! Her perfect automobile sits outside in the valet parking, and her perfect nails tap softly on the tablecloth.

At last her food arrives. To reassure her that she is a goddess, it must be just the right portion arranged perfectly on exactly the right kind of plate. Its ingredients must be politically correct and its description on the menu must be properly worded. Nothing else will do. She is a goddess.

She knows that she *deserves* to be with other gods and goddesses in a room fit for them and them alone. The whole atmosphere of the meal must be worthy of her or she simply "cannot eat." Sleek and elegant, she seems a far cry from some truck-stop customer shoveling down prodigious portions of chicken-fried steak and mashed potatoes. But I delight in both children equally. Both resemble me, their father.

The issue is not really food. That, in fact, is irrelevant. The point is the event of eating. Both of them turn to the moment of eating, not for fellowship or nourishment, but to celebrate their unlimited divinity. They are Bacchus, the fat, jolly god of more, and Diana, the sleek, warrior-goddess of beauty, both demanding worship.

✖✖

The issue is not really food.
That, in fact, is irrelevant.
The point is the event of eating.

✖✖

The meal is a sacrament and the waiters are priests. The sacrifice of the food, whether served in shapeless globs or laid gently on a bed of romaine, is nonetheless a sacrifice. "You cannot be limited. You are without laws or boundaries," I whisper. "You are a goddess of perfection." I urge her to demand perfection. Mortals have heart attacks, not gods. More! More! More!

The Tyrant speaks of a last supper. But I served the first supper in the Garden. "Take and eat," I said, "this is my body given for you and for many. Suck out the forbidden juice. It is blood of a new covenant, that you may be a goddess."

And the woman did eat of the fruit and she gave it to her husband and their eyes were opened as from a deep sleep. They knew that they were divine. Everything, absolutely everything, from that moment on was food for the gods.

"Eat *more* in remembrance of me, as oft as ye shall eat."

꘎꘎

CHAPTER THIRTEEN

Michael Answers Concerning Gluttony

A h, at last, the mask of sophistication slips. Now, Professor, you begin to see Lucifer as he is—Evil with crumbs on its face. He is the devourer. He is a bloody lion with crimson fangs and gory claws. He is a thief who rips to shreds whatever he steals, a murderer who devours whatever he kills.

He loves to dress up in robes of self-righteous propriety and sit benignly with the finest guests at the best tables. But he simply cannot hide his ravenous, carnivorous beastliness. When he leaves a place, it is always littered with carnage.

Lucifer fans the flames of insatiable appetite. He drives poor neurotic girls to gorge or starve themselves to death and then laughs at their gullible quest for fullness.

Anorexics and bulimics are not gluttons for food but for control. They want something, anything they control. They are not so much gluttons as they are pathetic victims of Lucifer's Gluttony. He would devour *them.*

He screams "More, more!" in the ears of the satiated and makes the full belly feel empty. He loves to look calm, controlled, cool, and urbane. But he is actually a furtive, ravenous wolf tearing at the bodies of his own overfed, porcine victims, while his bloody red eyes dart back and forth seeking whom else he may devour.

He himself eats and eats and eats. His kingdom is more about Gluttony than mortals can imagine. He feeds the flesh so that his demons may feed on the flesh.

In his Gluttony, Lucifer's charade of jaded, cosmopolitan disinterest is exposed. He is no well-dressed party guest, halfheartedly nibbling dainties from a saucer. He is a devourer. He will not wait. He will not share. He will not divide. He has no manners or morals. He devours.

Heaven agrees with Lucifer on one thing, at least. The sin of Gluttony is not totally about food. Gluttony is an idolatry of eating. The act of putting food into one's mouth becomes a sensual worship of the barest order when Gluttony sets in on a life.

As Lucifer himself has pointed out in his perverse ramblings, Gluttony has two faces. The one is of that formless, gross company of gorgers. The other face is of the gourmets. They seem contrary to one another, but they are conjoined at the belly.

The first face we might call "classical" gluttony, if I may use such an adjective to describe such a disgusting sin. This traditional concept of Gluttony is what most humans envision when they dare to contemplate the sin at all.

> *The sin of Gluttony is not totally about food.*
> *Gluttony is an idolatry of eating.*

Gluttony's more obvious form takes little or no interest in food's color, taste, or preparation. Since Gluttony is not about food, it cares nothing for delicacies. It has no time for graciousness. Manners are a hateful oppression to Gluttony because they are laws to keep eating sane.

Bon Appetit is a meaningless phrase to the glutton of this first school. Appetite implies some sense of desire for the food itself, but this glutton has never hungered and has never lacked the desire to eat. For him the food need not be appetizing. And it can hardly be bland or tasteless or even revolting enough to take his appetite. *Bon Appetit* indeed! The German *Essen Gut* (good eating) is more like it. But even that Teutonic benediction causes a shrug of his shoulders. What can that mean? Is there bad eating? He knows no value system. There is only eating.

The glutton has lost the link between food and life. He does not eat to live; he does not even live to eat. Eating defines his life. Such Gluttony makes him graceless in more than one way. There is no need to say "grace" over what he does. Incoherent to him is the plea, "Give us this day our daily bread."

Your Redeemer Kinsman taught you that prayer because he knew you needed constant reminding of your dependence upon God for life. "Give us life today." That is the prayer Jesus taught. Give us life this day because we depend upon You, the Lord of Life. Today, this day, give us what we need to live.

But how can the glutton pray such a prayer? He does not eat food. He eats eating itself. He can hardly lean upon God for sustenance. Graceless and without gratitude, he knows nothing of depending on the Lord of life. His belly is his god and he eats death unto death.

Because food is not really the issue, nourishment and satisfaction are irrelevant. Hence, there is no thought of amount or sufficiency or concern for others. The Gluttony of the West is a twisted form of cannibalism. Rather than eating dead flesh, such Gluttony eats flesh to death. When a man consistently eats much more than is good for *his* life, the very fact of his eating is bad for someone else's life. He actually eats the life of someone somewhere who has less than life requires. Gluttony is dead men eating themselves to death while others starve. Is it any wonder Gluttony is a deadly sin?

Gluttony is deadly not only in its connection to obesity and heart disease. It is also deadly independence. Gluttony is the hand-to-mouth rebellion that refuses the basic law of God: "Thou shalt *love* the Lord thy God with all they heart and mind and soul and strength." Gluttony skewers obedience on a knife and fork. It fillets faith and coats humility in jam.

The tears of angels fall like rain at the tragic loneliness of Gluttony. It is the loneliest of all the deadly sins.

What this lying Lucifer will not tell you is the loneliness of Gluttony. He loves Gluttony and calls it a virtue. But he will *not* tell you about the isolation. There sits the traveling salesman in his motel room, the table before him littered with half-empty cartons of take-out Chinese food. He stares blankly at the flickering images on the television and methodically shovels down prodigious mouthfuls of lukewarm *moo goo gai pan*.

Hunger eludes him. He cannot remember ever being hungry. He is not even driven by food. It owns him dully. As he sits alone in his room, fellowship is swallowed up by a mechanized separation. His contact with life has no more depth than the flat creatures on his TV screen. There may have been a time when he enjoyed the evening's relaxation in the solitude of a motel. Somewhere far in his past there may have even been a moment where he savored the taste of a foreign delicacy. Now it is gone. He has eaten himself out of house and home. No conversation. No interaction. No thought. No life. No joy. Over the lips, over the gums... look out, stomach, here it comes. The tasteless globs enter his mouth one after the other like bags of garbage on some dumpster's conveyor belt. One, two, three, four. Switch the channel and eat some more.

The tears of angels fall like rain at the tragic loneliness of Gluttony. It is the loneliest of all the deadly sins.

Lucifer tells men they are gods. Does he thus make them free? Hardly! He steals their very humanity and leaves them wallowing alone in the pigsty. The prodigal would gladly have filled his belly with the food of pigs. These are gods? Pathetic!

Gluttony's other face is more attractive, but it is no less an obsession. Is pathological disgust with fat any healthier than a pathological lust for it? The health food addict is an absurd carica- ture. His food fetishes are dogmatic self-exaltations. He is an elit- ist who constantly celebrates his own body. He says he is about health, but he is deceived. He is all about himself. He pets, exer- cises, dresses, and feeds his own body as if it were other than him- self.

Such a glutton constantly searches for a better wheat germ or a better tofu or a better piece of exercise equipment. He pours over catalogs, searching for one more specialty food or dietary secret to assure him that his body is receiving the best.

Strangely enough, he may use Scripture to justify his obsession. He speaks in broad terms of not abusing the "temple," but he is a true idolater. Forgetting the Creator, he worships the temple. Far from glorifying God in his body, he glorifies himself. *He* is slim. *He* eats right (correctly—as in lawfully). *He* not only exercis- es but does the right, "acceptable" exercise. *He* deserves it. *He,* as a wholly other god, is the object of his worship.

The fascination is gluttonous. After a while it ceases to be about being healthy but about health *food*.

The gourmet is much the same. She does not eat caviar because she is hungry, but because it is *caviar.* She is an elitist who uses food for self-worship. Exotic foods convince her that she is rightfully among the elite. She is a connoisseur of wines not because she is addicted to alcohol, but because she is addicted to the expensive *and* to the private delight of knowing things hid- den from the masses.

The condescension of a gourmet is Gluttony. So is the revulsion the thin feel at being near a fat person. Both substitute eating for the security and comfort which God only should supply. Eating soothes, comforts, and rewards (blesses) them for being what they tell themselves they are—gods.

Their self-idolatry steers them carefully into deception and bondage. Knowing this, Lucifer makes them slaves by telling them they are gods.

Imagine two women thrust together by circumstance. They stare ferociously at one another across the expanse of a doctor's waiting room. How has fate been so cruel as to put them in such close quarters? The slimmer woman feels her stomach churning at the sight of the fat one's bulges and rolls. The fat woman sniffs at the skin and bones across the room and curses the discomfort she feels at the strange condescension and pity she sees in the other woman's eyes.

Later in their own apartments, each shudders as if to shake off the memory of the other. Fat sits down to an open carton of ice cream. Not even bothering to dip it into a dish, she eagerly eats huge spoonfuls, stopping only to gulp milk straight from a plastic jug. She ignores the widening pool of melting ice cream spreading out on the table. She ignores the dribbles speckling her dress. Eat! Eat! More! More!

She must be comforted. The sight of that skinny witch at the doctor's office must be buried under an avalanche—not of food but of eating. Unwatched, unchecked, unjudged, she gobbles the ice cream like a starving child. Yet, she hardly tastes it. It is the eating which comforts her.

Across town, Thin carefully slices the crust away from dry toast. She then cuts that into fourths and carefully arranges the tiny triangles on a silver caviar dish. She spoons the wet black beads into the center and pours exactly three fingers of wine into a crystal glass. Placing the dish and the glass on her dining table, she dims the lights and delicately caresses the crystal stem. As Frank Sinatra serenades her from the surround-sound system, her equilibrium returns. The nightmare in the doctor's office begins to dim as she allows the first swallow of wine to slide silkily down her throat. She dabs at the caviar with a corner of the toast. She feels so full she doubts that she can eat. The very sight of the perfect little evening snack before her proves as great a comfort as she had thought it would.

She knows that across this great city only a very special few ever sit just exactly as she does now—only the perfect ones who know what it means to sit fondling a wine glass and being fondled ever so gently by the voice of Old Blue Eyes. She nibbles at a corner of the toast. The saltiness of the caviar is perfect. She sighs and closes her eyes.

The fascination with the drug of choice soon becomes an absorption with the paraphernalia, the nomenclature, and culture associated with their lord and master.

The odd thing about all this to angels is that the two women are twins. They embarrass one another, but they both horrify the angels equally. How odd that humans see at such a surface level.

Gluttony is a deadly sin. All who yield to it are deadened to life, to themselves, and to God. The drug addict is a glutton. The alcoholic is a glutton. The fascination with the drug of choice soon becomes an absorption with the paraphernalia, the nomenclature, and culture associated with their lord and master. Like a dog chasing its tail, an addict cannot tell if he is enjoying the high or merely waiting for it to wear off so he can again experience *getting high*. Gluttons are no more excited about food than a junkie is about crack. Rather, they are bound by it.

The fastidious Pharisees were gluttons. They were unable to say, "He brings me to his banqueting table and his banner over me is love." They took no joy in the feast, nor did they benefit from a fast. They had no notion of God's love. Their incessant rituals of washing disgusted heaven. To the angels they appeared to be washing their hands in blood.

Just so gluttons always devour all that delights. They cannot have their joy and devour it too. O Jesu, joy of man's desiring; Thou and Thy sacrifice are wasted on the gluttons among the sons and daughters of Adam.

Lucifer hurls epithets at the Holy Meal. Let him. The children of God kneel down to eat at a table of grace, and grace upon grace rests sweetly upon every other table where they sit. How ironic indeed that those who reject the Lord's Supper find only emptiness and devouring in every other meal. But the meek who find mysterious fullness in bread and wine experience joy and fellowship at tables both simple and grand. "Come and dine," the Master calleth. "Come and dine."

Dialogue VII:

Lucifer: One of your last lines, "They cannot have joy and eat too," is the difference between me and the Tyrant. I say they *can* eat *and* have joy.

Michael: Must you misquote *everything*?

Lucifer: Where? What? I must have got it very nearly right. Perhaps some minor slip. I assure you it was . . .

Michael: What I said was, "They cannot have their joy and devour it too."

Lucifer: But what about the joy *of* devouring?

Michael: There *is* no joy in it. Joy has no destruction. And destruction gives no joy. Joy is never undisciplined. Joy has no desperation or selfishness or lust in it. Friends may sit and share a meal. They may even feast. Heaven is not miserly and joyless, doling out crusts of bread to be nibbled with a guilty conscience. In the feasts of the King, there is fullness of joy. But wolves devour. They devour the fallen stag, the wounded church, each other, and all hope of joy.

Lucifer: To feast or to devour—mere semantics.

Michael: No, Lucifer. Unless the difference between heaven and hell is mere semantics. When the sons and daughters of Adam begin to devour, they consume until they are consumed. Lost in the devouring is the love and fellowship and joy.

Lucifer: The Tyrant is about fasting. Tell the truth.

Michael: *About* fasting? Certainly not. True fasting *is* a feast, and spiritual feasting has many of the blessings of a fast. The King meets His children at both tables. But the devourers—they meet Him not at all. They drag their prey from His presence and tear it with merciless teeth. His children pray into His presence and feast on His mercy. They delight in His bread, because they are bred for His delight.

Lucifer: They are weaklings! Whoever will not devour shall be devoured.

Michael: The devourers are devoured, but fasted weaklings shall eat at a table He prepares while you are made to stand and watch!

Lucifer: Food and sex. Why is the Tyrant so frightened of these delights? Could it be that he is afraid that Lust may make a god or two besides himself?

Michael: Food and sex were *made* by Him. Gluttony and Lust are your bastard offspring.

Lucifer: Lust is last.

Michael: It usually is.

CHAPTER FOURTEEN

Lucifer on Lust

I am the animal god. I am the golden calf who caused the Hebrews to cast off tyranny and bondage and dance naked in the sands of Sinai. I am *Eros*. I painted lurid pictures on the walls of Roman whorehouses. I am *Pan* and the *Satyrs* who preyed on the forest nymphs. I am the animal god who stirs the loins and fires the brain. I have cloven hooves and woolen flanks and the lust of a billy goat. I rut like a boar and will not be denied. I am the animal god and the god of animals.

I have tried to reason with you. I have coaxed and cajoled and taught. I am a reasonable god, but I am weary of this game. Michael, this chilly star of heaven's frozen tyranny, smugly trots out all his platitudes and picture postcards of my "pathetic victims." How about that sad scene of lonely gluttons eating their hearts out? What a ludicrous effort to answer the power of my divine reason!

But if this game must be played that way, then let us have the gloves off. I know what heaven will say. My earth, I've heard it enough. Well, let them say it. Let us hear all their mumbo jumbo about sex being holy and men not being beasts, and their farcical, cutsie-pie fairy stories about virgin births that make a lie of it all. I can tell you now that's what Michael will say. Let it be said. It changes nothing.

Let me tell you a thing or two about one of the sweetest of all virtues—Lust. It is far more profound than you may imagine. Do not begin with sweaty teenagers groping each other in the backseat of a car. Also, forget brothels for now, though they are not nearly what the Tyrant would have you think. Instead, look at some of my finest work—the classrooms! There is my true masterpiece of Lust. The Tyrant wants to weave this holy mystique around sex. He wants to separate man from the animals. But I have made a miracle. Biology professors inspired by me have accomplished what a million prostitutes and a flood of pornography could never have done.

My mind behind theirs—that is the secret. The mind behind the mind. Together we shifted the compass needle of the Western world from due north to dead south. We taught a generation that they were animals!

Biology professors inspired by me have accomplished what a million prostitutes and a flood of pornography could never have done.

You gape! Are you blind? Or deaf? I said *animals!* A generation of animal-gods. A whole generation became gods. Self-made, or at least the accidents of time, they saw no authority to which they must bow. Without authority, they had no explanation beyond themselves and each other.

Like dogs and cats and mice, this generation was free at last to enjoy their own gods. Who could rule them? What rules could restrict them?

The reasoning was direct and simple: If there is no creator, then man is free to be a god. If a god, then a beast. The Tyrant's image obliterated, the serial numbers rubbed out, the New Thing rose *yet again* from rebel of tyranny. Cain and Caligula were not just reformed humans. Humanism is not a new idea. "Behold old things have passed away, all things become new."

The New Thing now rules in my stead. He rules the schools with a gun in his hand. She rules the bedrooms and boardrooms, using sex as a weapon. She rules her own body and slaughters the fruit of her womb. He rules with rape. The New Thing dances nude on a million barroom tables. The New Thing does exactly as he pleases.

Creator, redeemer, and sustainer I am! I am the god of the New Thing. Mere creations were human beings, the animated figurines of a mad sculptor until *I* came along. *I* created freedom. *I* redeemed humanity from creation. *I* sustain humanity by flesh and spirit. By my constant, unflagging zeal, I convince them over and over and over again:

You are a beast! Take what you lust for.

You are a god! Rape if you please.

You are a god-beast! Lust is the holy venom in the fangs of your loins. Strike and be pleased.

Now I am warming to the subject. Lust is the virtue that makes a god an animal. Without it a god is bound by the most prosaic of limitations. Antique concepts such as loyalty make mice of gods. How can a god be bound by such chains? The Tyrant cloaks his viciousness in words like *covenant, relationship,* and, worst of all, *family.*

I despise his attempts to draw the fangs from my gods. The greatest of all blasphemies is to deny a god his own divinity.

The little professor seems to be a bit confused. Does this sound a great deal like gluttony? Of course!

Lust unlimited is the very lifeblood of a god. Through his veins pulses an undeniable river of hot lava that melts everything in its path. What dares to say no to the Lust of a god? Shall a woman? Hah! An insignificant child? Blasphemy! Incest? A mere word designed to hem in gods. What an utterly ridiculous idea! The lava of Lust leaps such pathetic little barriers. Nay, it consumes them by the molten wrath of a god. Pedophile, necrophile, nymphomaniac, rapist, adulterer, homosexual, lesbian, or pornographer—call them whatever you like—they are gods in the earth.

✖✖

*The reasoning was direct and simple:
If there is no creator, then man is free to be a god.
If a god, then a beast.*

✖✖

I have placed Lust last on my list of great virtues, but it is by no means the least of my concerns. By it many a man and woman has learned of their divinity. As their flesh stirred and tingled, they felt the throbbing pulse of the divine within them. I spoke only in unison with their own flesh and in concert with the sexual world around them. The world, their flesh, and ME—the triune godhead of Lust. Three in one! Let the Tyrant match that!

Come back with me to old Jerusalem to see how the virtue of Lust can set a man free to be a god. David, for all his failures, very nearly became a god in the arms of sweet Lust.

As the King stands on his balcony, the cool night breeze stirs the hair on his forearms. The expensive material of his lounging robe softly caresses his body and the twinkling lights of Jerusalem stretch far below him. He is King. He is adored by his army, his guards, and his nation.

I am there. I stand behind him massaging his ego with practiced fingers. I whisper in the breeze. The rustling of fig leaves sounds at first like, "You are king, king, king." Then it blurs softly into "God, god, god. You are god." My sheep hear my voice and follow me.

Ah! She appears. My timing is excellent. Pardon my lack of

false humility. It's just that timing is one of my best things. I can tell when a man is ready to claim his own divinity and just when to provide him with the perfect instrument of liberation.

Bathsheba, daughter of delight, shimmers in the moonlight. Her silvery limbs are lent a supernatural glow as the sponge releases its delicious rivers. David's eyes are riveted. His pulse pounds. Lips parted, he breathes in short gasps, sucking air across dry lips. Then it occurs to him, "Why should I deny myself? I am king. Her king. To whom shall I answer?" Power, luxury, and Lust flow together in raging confluence. The chrysalis of his damp divinity stirs, rustling its wings against the cocoon of law and tradition.

"Thou shalt not commit adultery."

The thought flicks across his mind, the Tyrant's desperate attempt to impose his will on the Lust of a god. What despicable oppression!

It is easily dealt with. Bathsheba lifts her hair with both hands. Elbows akimbo, eyes closed, she is a milk-white statue of incredible promise. *Her* pose at *that* moment on *that* rooftop, and the butterfly of David's divinity erupts from its moral shell and sheds the useless thing. Unseen even by him, the mind of self-ownership rises full grown behind him and spreads its wings in the moonlight.

"Bring her to me," he tells his guard. "Bring Bathsheba, the wife of Uriah."

In the natural realm, a whispered command in the simplest of human words. But the voice behind the voice is mine. The mind behind the mind is mine. I am the god who makes kings into gods.

David's whispered command was a howl heard deep within the heavenlies. It was the primordial scream of outrage. The tyranny of heaven was broken and the king became a god.

I am the god of Lust. Bring the firstborn to ME. The Tyrant

tries to connect sex with life, but sex is about Lust, not life. Beast with beast. Uncreated god with uncreated god. I am Molech. I am the Canaanite god of fire. I am he to whom they sacrifice through their infant offerings. Bring the firstborn to ME! The firstborn is mine. And I AM the god of fire.

And David took the woman. He did not *know* her. He *took* her in lust; white, hot passion as undeniable as the will of any god. And the woman conceived and brought forth, and my armies informed me. Unto you this day in the palace of David a child is born, a son is given. And his father wrapped him in swaddling clothes and laid him in a coffin.

CHAPTER FIFTEEN

Michael Answers Concerning Lust

Finally, Lucifer shows himself for what he is—Apollyon, the author of death and destruction. He steals, kills, and destroys. He is the confuser. He makes sin righteousness and righteousness sin. He is a liar and the father of all lies. But ultimately, his makeup always runs. Slick and soft-spoken at the first, he comes not with brutality, but with philosophy and vain deceit. He cunningly justifies himself and the children of wrath.

He is a word-monger who twists all words and especially the Word of God. He sails in under any flag that will admit him to port, but he cannot hide the truth for long.

Lucifer is no sophisticated modern professor of fresh moral concepts. He is the bloodthirsty Molech who prowled Hinnon among the caves of the Canaanites. He is a dragon, the serpent of monstrous evil. He is the cosmic adulterer and the lord of Lust. His children bear his mark on their foreheads and on their hands.

It is his lack of patience that finally shows him up. He will not wait. He cannot delay gratification. So now, here he is at the end and his urbane sophistry degenerates into the final tactic of the rapist. See how all his lies seemed so smooth at the first? Now he shows the talons beneath.

How strange it is to the angels that the most obvious of Lucifer's lies is the most believable to modern mortals. The sin of

Lust destroys sex and life. Yet mortals continue to believe Lust is the secret to happiness in sex and fullness of life.

As in every area, Lucifer comes but to steal, kill, and destroy. For all his condescending sophistication and his smug Playboy cartoons, Lucifer cannot hide the sheer destruction of Lust. He cannot hide AIDS under a veneer of smutty jokes by TV comedians. Lucifer cannot make a demonized rapist inflamed by pornography into anything but the horror he is. Lucifer cannot clean up the malignant nightmare of Lust.

Lust steals the joy of human sexuality. Lust destroys homes, families, consciences, and minds. And... Lust kills.

Among the other six of the deadly sins, Lust is most related to Gluttony. As Gluttony is not about food, Lust is not about love. An addict "does" drugs, a glutton "does" food, and Lust "does" sex.

✖✖

Lust steals the joy of human sexuality. Lust destroys homes, families, consciences, and minds. And... Lust kills.

✖✖

There is nothing relational about Lust. Gluttons are isolated in the act of eating; they do not enjoy the others at the table. In the same way, the lustful are isolated in the act of sex: The Father's original plan in His creation of sexuality, which involves one "knowing" another, eludes the desperation of sex. Love wants to know, Lust wants to use. To the gluttonous, food is a tool for eating; to the lustful, another person is only a body, an instrument of sex.

Like Gluttony, Lust is lonely. Its loneliness is pride or self-love. Intimacy is not possible without relationship with another. Masturbation is solitary, pornography is lonely, and adultery lacks committed relationship.

At the end of masturbation is the ache of emptiness, not calm fulfillment. Pornography steals the warm touch and leaves a cold slick color photograph. Pornography is incomprehensible to angels. It is one-dimensional Lust.

Adultery is equally empty and unfulfilling. Adulterers leave by separate doors, pretend not to know one another at parties, and avoid eye contact. Adultery enforces an excruciating loneliness that hangs up without answering and jerks away its hand. Lust is lonely.

The greater problem with Lust, however, is that in getting its object, nothing is "settled." Lust fulfilled "has" nothing. It must immediately start over. Hence, the law of diminishing return drives the lustful ever closer to the brink of sexual burnout. Jaded and seared, the lustful must constantly veer deeper into the bizarre and twisted for titillation.

Lust fulfilled "has" nothing,
It must immediately start over.

A yielding to Lust steals the very thing that Lucifer promises it will grant—sexual fulfillment. What an odd paradox that the jaded will laugh at the "family values and corn-fed wholesomeness" of others, while he himself becomes impotent without photos of bestiality and pitiful little children. By gradually deadening himself, he must constantly go to more and more desperate lengths to be sexually stimulated. But the square "John Boy" next door, with three kids and a station wagon, tingles in sexual anticipation at his wife's tender touch, or her meaningful wink when the kids aren't watching.

Lucifer is the devourer and Lust devours. There is a subterranean Satanic impulse resident in Lust. It is the urge of a small boy who, not content to see a lovely blossom, crushes it and grinds it between his palms. Lust craves for what it is not possible to "have." The language of Lust is possessive, yet the reality is that sex gains nothing. A man cannot "have" a woman in sex, nor she him, but the craving remains.

Lust sees youthful innocence—even the innocence of childhood—and wants to "have" it. Unable to do so, the impulse of Lust is to crush it. Lust wants to grind the blossom against its face. Lust longs to force beauty in through its own pores. An obsession with deflowering virgins is but the monstrous perversion of a longing to "have" what Lust demands.

The voracious appetite of Lust makes everyone its victim. The seduced child is the victim of the Lust of the pedophile. The ruined virgin is the victim of the rapacious Lust of her date. The prostitute is the victim of the Lust of her customer. How strange to angels that humans speak of Lust as being a sin with no victims. Lust has more victims than wrath.

Often those who are the prey of the lustful also prey upon the lustful. Lust steals judgment and exposes the otherwise reasonable to great danger. The lustful businessman preys on a drug-dependent prostitute barely out of her teens. He, in turn, is exposed to AIDS, scandal, violence, and robbery. Lust drives men to make and become victims of its hellish power.

The worst of Lust's larceny, however, is its ability to steal reality from its victims. Through Lust, they sink into a horrible swamp of nightmare images and sickening shades that slide across the stage of their minds. Reality dies in the fumes of evil imaginations. Torture, violence, carnality, and sensuality bubble up from dead underground pools so noxious that nothing real can grow on the banks. Humanity perishes and ghouls fill the air. Discernment, beauty, life, and joy all lie poisoned on the banks of these contaminated reservoirs of Lust. The Lust to "know" was the very desire which led Eve to eat the death fruit in the first place. Yet, in the lethal fumes of the pools of Lust, the knowledge of the difference between good and evil dies horribly and forever.

The lustful cannot tell the difference between real and imaginary. Truth and falsehood change places. The holy and the corrupt first blend, then separate topside down, when Lust enters in.

Lust sees everything at its own level. It discerns no value in chastity, no beauty in love, and no worth at all in sex. Lust denounces the Creator as imaginary, deifies its daydreams as gods, and bathes humanity in bestial worthlessness. Lust makes life and people as one-dimensional as pornographic photos and denies the existence of the Holy One of Israel.

I remember Sodom! Ask Lucifer about Gomorrah. Go out and see the saline basin of death where once stood prosperous centers of commerce. Gaze upon the sterile sea of death and the stench of Lust with which Sodom and Gomorrah once filled the air, and there demand an answer of Lucifer: "Where are they now who abandoned beauty, soul, and sanity to Lust?"

I remember being there. We went down for Lot who had pitched his tent toward Sodom. I remember the horror of men like reservoir dogs, men without eyes, men who could not tell angels from whores. And we saw men without ears who could not hear the voice of heaven. We went down to rescue Lot and saw cities gone mad with Lust. The men of Sodom lusted for us angels. Lust would rape heaven as well as earth.

Lust destroys the humanity of humans. Beasts like the monsters of Sodom lurk in the murky waters of Lust's deadly pools. I remember a city of such perversion and wickedness that men made rape an art and lost their ability to tell heaven from hell. Let Lucifer tell the truth about Sodom. Stand on the alkaline sands of a lifeless sea and stare at massive pillars of saline death and demand of Lucifer the truth. Walk the halls of AIDS wards and weep at the whimpers of dying boys.

The thief cometh but to steal and to kill and to destroy. The mask is altogether off now. The game is up. The wages of sin is death.

The history of the Seven Deadly Sins is written in the polluted blood of a fallen race. "Lucifer! Rebel. Liar. Destroyer. Apollyon. Father of lies. Yours is the history of death."

But there is a balm in Gilead.

Dialogue VIII

Lucifer: I'm through with this.

Michael: Of course. It's over. That's all seven.

Lucifer: I think I've proven my point. The seven deadly "sins" are actually virtues. The Tyrant wants to be the only god; by calling godly virtues sin, he keeps men in bondage.

Michael: The King would make them sons.

Lucifer: Riddle me this. If the Tyrant would allow them to be sons of God, then why not gods?

Michael: That is the line which can never be crossed. Angels are angels. They can stay in heaven or fall like lightning, but they can never be gods. At the crossing of that line all death enters in. The sons of God may not become or aspire to be gods. That is death.

Lucifer: That is divinity and I have many gods. Even in his church. Proud, fierce, unruled, self-willed, greedy, slothful, glorious gods. They teach one another to become gods. They live above his laws and destroy his servants and invent pleasures unto themselves in his name. They laugh when he weeps and weep when he laughs. They speak as gods of their own desires, and in envious wrath wreck havoc in his house. Mine! Mine, mine, mine! And they do not even know it. What sublime delight. They think because they do not worship me that they are not of me. I care nothing for their worship. I only want them to be gods. For I am god and the god of all gods; all gods are of me.

Michael: You? You are defined only as "not what you were." You are the fallen one. Unredeemable. Unrepentant. Rebel. The fire awaits you. Nothing else. But for them there is still hope. There is a balm in Gilead. Goodbye, Lucifer.

Lucifer: Shall we not meet again? I do so love our little chats.

Michael: Meet again? To be sure, but not for a chat. At God's command, our brother Gabriel shall lift the trump and summon you to your reward.

Lucifer: I am god! I am. I am. I AM!

CHAPTER SIXTEEN

Take Up and Read

"And you," Lucifer shouted at me, "you have been a great disappointment. How did someone so gullible and stupid ever become an astronomy professor? I feel sorry for your students, but I am not sorry for you. You're a pathetic old failure. You are a nothing. No one will ever know your name. But MINE they know! I am god. Do *not* expect wages. There are no wages for you!"

Turning his eyes on Michael he continued the harangue. He was obviously out of control.

"And you, you," he screamed, jabbing the air between them with his forefinger, "you are an immoral, deceitful emissary of a monstrously wicked Tyrant. You are the plenipotentiary of heaven's fallenness. You—you liar! You thief! You destroyer of gods! This entire debate—"

Only then did Michael interrupt. "I told you from the beginning that there would be no debate. This was never a debate."

"How dare you!" Lucifer screamed. "Who do you think you are?"

"A messenger," Michael said softly. "Who do you think you are? That is more nearly the question."

With that Lucifer uttered a shriek of such rage and ferocious volume that I involuntarily brought my hands to my ears. Seeing my gesture, Lucifer laughed. Turning to Michael with one last disdainful glare, he laughed even louder. Throwing his head back, his laughter became a frightening howl. Then he was gone. There was no cinematic puff of smoke and no room-rattling explosion. Just a burst of derisive laughter, an eerie howl, and he was gone.

Nothing had ever so thoroughly shaken me as this night's events. I laid my head back against the chair and closed my eyes. My hands fell limply to either side of the computer.

Lucifer's words continued to echo in my brain. "You're a pathetic old failure! Failure. Failure. You're nothing. Nothing. Nothing. Nothing! No one will ever know your name. And you will never be paid any wages."

I knew it was true. Utter fatigue clawed my body and brain downward. The sleepless night of labor hurled me ruthlessly onto the anvil of lassitude. But Lucifer's words echoing in my mind were the destroying hammer. I wanted to never open my eyes again. I wanted to go back to my safe, sleepy, undisturbed university cocoon. But I knew that it had been forever destroyed. Lucifer and, in his own way, Michael, had stolen my tidy little life.

I was more tired than I had ever been or had ever known a man could be. I felt the weight of my own useless failure-hood settling in upon me like a corporeal fog.

I squinted my eyes more tightly against a sudden scraping noise and an unwelcome bath of light against my eyelids. Even with my eyes tightly closed, I could sense the wavelike variations in light, as if someone had stepped between me and a bright light. I cracked my eyes open just enough to let the brilliant flash of sunlight crash inward.

The scene confused me. Shielding my eyes with my right hand and peeling away my bifocals with my left, I squinted at the scene like the silly old mole I must have resembled. Light cascaded in rippling shafts around a figure positioned directly between me and the large floor-length window across from my desk. I realized that someone, Michael I supposed, had drawn back the drapes and the morning sun was streaming into the little room. The imposing figure between me and the window was a faceless shadow around which the shafts of sunlight shot in a painful display of power.

"He's lying, of course," Michael said.

"What?" I asked.

"Lucifer. He always does. He is father of all lies. He lied all night. But that last bit, that felt different to you, didn't it?"

"Yes," I said, dropping my head like a schoolboy caught in some shameful little scandal.

"But it's a lie, Professor. You are not a nothing."

"No," I whined. "He's right. I've nothing to show for my life. My name will never be—"

"Your name? Forget that. The Prince of Glory is the only Name that matters."

"I'm so tired," I said, suddenly unable to even keep my eyes open.

"Yes," Michael said. "Rest is what you need."

"I don't suppose I shall be paid. I suppose he's right about that. There are no wages for me."

"Ask not for wages," Michael said. "Rest is what you need."

"Yes," I said, as I again laid my head back onto the chair. "Rest. O God—how can I . . .?"

I fell off to sleep like a man falling over a cliff. The last thing I heard Michael say was, "Just take up and read. Take up and read. There on the screen. Look on the screen, Professor."

Then he was gone. And so was I. I fell into the deepest sleep of my entire life. It must have been several hours later when the housekeeper shook me awake.

"Professor," she said, shaking my arm. "Professor, please wake up!"

"Yes," I said, lifting my head. My neck had cramped in an awkward position and I winced. "Oh, Mrs. Adamson! It's you. My! Oh, my neck."

"Are you all right?" She asked. "I've been shaking you and calling you for five minutes. I was just going for help. You frightened me."

"No. No, I'm fine. I—well—I worked all night."

"Professor, I think you need rest," she said.

"What did you say?" I asked her in astonishment.

"Why, rest, Professor. You need rest."

"Yes," I muttered under my breath. "I do."

My computer screen was still on. Printed there were only these words arranged on the screen just as you see them here:

Romans 6:23   Hebrews 4:9

Matthew 11:28

Take Up and Read

A Final Word

I read someplace that upon completing the *Screwtape Letters*, C.S. Lewis said that writing it had been the worst struggle of his career. There are statements like that which one blithely reads, makes casual note of, and promptly ignores, only to realize later that they were pregnant with caution.

Writing this book has been a terrifying experience. In order to catch a bear, hunters say one must think like a bear. I grossly underestimated how wrenching it is to intentionally think like hell. That is not to say that my mind is unaccustomed to hellish thoughts. Quite the contrary. But I am now convinced that even the most devilish thoughts can parade through our minds quite without analysis. That is to say, we may think them but refuse to look at them for what they are, refuse to recognize the clear stamp of Satan upon them. To deliberately descend into the abyss is quite another thing altogether.

I wanted to teach on sin by "turning the world top-side down," as it were. I reasoned that by letting Lucifer talk, he would talk himself into the grave. To stretch the metaphor, I wanted the devil to take enough rope to hang himself.

The dual shock to my own system was what I underestimated. The first and perhaps more predictable blow was the vicious counterattack from the enemy.

Now, please understand. I have never been overly enthusiastic about the understanding of spiritual warfare that is emphasized in some circles. It seems to me that some who actively engage in this type of warfare do so to excess. However, over the course of the year which it took me to write this book, every doorknob seemed intent upon breaking off in my hand. Spiritual struggles, deep personal disappointments, and stunning disillusionment dogged my steps. And the effort to actually turn the notes and research into prose became a fierce internal struggle. No other book I have ever attempted fought me like this one did.

I knew, of course, that the face behind the glittering mask of satanic deception would be hideous. I wanted a book that exposes sin for what it really is. The media, our culture, and our nature *want* to believe the deception. We love the mask. We do not want it snatched off any more than Lucifer does. The beautiful camouflage comforts us that, after all, our lust and greed and wrath are not really all that bad.

Lucifer alone was too horrible, too perverted to bear. Hence, the "response of heaven" in Michael's voice. But Heaven will not compete with deception. God lets the lie wear all the glitter. The exotic lacquers on Lucifer's mask are designed to make the "unvarnished truth" seem dull and mundane.

God's truth, unvarnished as it is, is Heaven's only answer.

One older and wiser than I warned me that Lucifer will not lightly suffer his mask to be ripped away. Evil aims to drape itself in respectability. Indeed, Satan loves to claim moral superiority. To jerk away the drape and expose the bare bones of sin is an attack on hell. And hell fights back.

The second shock of writing this book, however, was not one which I could have predicted. The descent down the slippery staircase of madness is a harrowing experience. The labyrinthian maze of the twisted spirit, that calls evil righteous and God a tyrant, is a darksome nightmare of the soul even for the tourist.

I found it more agonizing than I imagined to think the Mad Hatter's thoughts. The self-justifying insanity of dogmatized sin seemed more evil to me, as I attempted to "let it speak its mind."

Then it dawned on me. That is the way it is. Hatred, wrath, and racism hide behind tradition, culture, and social mores. They do not seem terribly real in the faces we see at the local garden club. But after a few pages of *Mien Kampf,* our stomachs are churning. It is the stark expression of sin as righteousness and righteousness as sin that grabs us by the shoulders and brutally shakes us out of the afternoon nap of denial and self-defense.

The worst part of all was the horrifying realization that an utterly warped satanic spirit can indwell a life so average as to even be banal.

The shuddering, spine-tingling nightmare of the concentration camps was not that the guards observed and participated in these atrocities. The truly grisly thought is that those men went home and kissed their wives and tossed their children in the air and bought birthday presents for their mothers. The most gruesome reality in the universe is sin. Not only is it an offense to heaven, and a monstrosity that makes men into moral aberrants, but it does so like a silent, deadly virus that disguises itself as normal life.

I had always thought of the Seven Deadly Sins as antiquities of our theological past. I considered the list itself some useless medieval effort at categorizing the trivial sins of that more innocent era. Yet, after a year of reading, studying, and writing, I am convinced that gluttony, for example, is not some irrelevant theological relic. It is near the very heart of a great deal that is badly wrong in modern society.

Sloth, greed (avarice), lust, and all the rest are general areas of sin, the comprehension of which is important. Only by identifying and boldly labeling our sins as exactly what they are will we be convicted, feel remorse, and repent. If I "have a bit of a temper," I do not see that as anything but the occasional unpropitious manifestation of macho image or female petulance. But if I face square on that I am guilty of the deadly sin of wrath, I must repent. I must! My shock and disgust at seeing Lucifer's fires in my own eyes will drive me into the arms of God only if I am properly horrified.

The universality of sin eases my conscience not at all. Indeed, the Bible points it out. "All have sinned..." (Rom 3:23). That in no way excuses *me*. It only means that I am an active and personally responsible participant in a cosmic rebellion that stretches behind the veil of space and time into the nether regions of heaven.

Jesus looked into the faces of hateful Pharisees and told them, "Ye are of your father, the devil, and the lusts of your father ye will do" (JN 8:44).

It is sin, deadly in all its forms, that is the curse of death. Lucifer is the father of sin, and in the end they will share his death. The gospel is a merciless mirror held firmly before us in which we may behold our lineage etched in our faces.

"We have sinned" is not the dehumanized and humiliated cry of a despairing race beaten beyond hope by pre-Renaissance legalists. "We have sinned" is the key to open heaven's heart for an outpouring of Calvary Love. It is the doorway to revival. It is the path of personal renewal and societal restoration.

Robbie Burns said, "Would some pow'r the giftie give us to see ourselves as ithers see us."

Nay! We must care not at all how *others* see us. But the gift of ruthless grace is to see my sin as *He* does. Only in the agony of that bitter revelation will I repent as He longs for me to do.

"If we confess our sins, He is faithful and just to forgive us our sins, and to cleanse us from all unrighteousness" (1 Jn 1:9).

Mark Rutland
1995

DATE DUE